CATHERINE
OF THE ERIE

CATHERINE

of the

ERIE

by

CLAUDIO R. SALVUCCI

ARX PUBLISHING
MERCHANTVILLE, NJ

Arx Publishing
Merchantville, New Jersey

First Edition

ISBN: 978-1-935228-32-5

Author's Note

What little we know of the life of Catherine Gandeaktena* is contained in the *Jesuit Relations*, the *Annual Narrative of the Mission of the Sault*, and the biographies of Kateri Tekakwitha. The key moments of her life are a matter of record. A few quotations of hers have even come down to us. Overall, I have made my best effort to retell her story as accurately as possible within the constraints of what remains to us, supplemented with other relevant stories from the *Relations*. When possible, and when I felt their dramatic impact could not be improved upon, I have used exact language and quotations from the original sources. All the same, I have felt at liberty to invent scenes when the narrative called for it—and I pray Catherine that these do her no disfavor.

—*CRS*

* Gandeaktena, and other forms with *Gand-*, are most common in the Jesuit Relations; the variations with *Gann-* rather than *Gand-* reflect Iroquois pronunciation. In modern Mohawk, her name is rendered *Kaneaktenha* (see *Kateri*, issue 79). The eminent historian Henry Béchard, S.J. found a Huron version *Annietenha* in a manuscript catalogue of the enrollees of the Confraternity of the Holy Family at Quebec. A myriad of spellings appear in older sources: the above seem to be legitimate linguistic variants, but others are simply mistakes. Forms that end in *-ewa* and *-eüa* probably came from mistaken transcriptions of Bruyas, who used *ü* to mark a nasal vowel. Her name was likely pronounced Gahn-day-ahk-TEN-ha, with the EN a nasal vowel just like French *en*. This is unnatural in English, however, so I have been in the habit of pronouncing it Gahn-day-AHK-ten-ah.

CHAPTERS

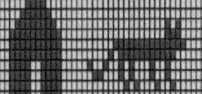

GENTAIENTON

June 1646.

The women of the Erie Nation were returning from the fields, some carrying their children and others carrying bark baskets full of little sweet strawberries. A year ago, the entire Erie nation had moved many miles inland from the great lake that bears their name. Now better protected from their enemies to the West, and closer to the lucrative trade routes on the Susquehanna and Delaware Rivers, this was the first Strawberry festival in their new village, and the town was excited and in high spirits.

One mother, carrying a toddler in her arms, pointed toward the village. "Gandeaktena, look!"

"Daddy!" she squealed with her arms out. Her mother let her down and she ran wildly to her father, her long black hair trailing behind her.

He waited outside the village with a pretend look of surprise on his face, his arms outstretched toward her. "Gotcha!" he laughed as he snatched her up and twirled her around. "And what have *you* been doing, little one?"

"We got *so* many strawberries, daddy!" she gestured back toward the women.

"So you do!" he laughed. "The spirits have blessed us!"

"I want strawberry syrup!"

"Oh you *do*, do you?" he lowered his brows in mock anger. "But no strawberry syrup until the feast starts. Now run back to the longhouse," he said, putting her down and swatting her behind, "and get ready." She sprinted away in excitement.

Her father loitered at the entrance as Gandeaktena's mother approached. "Someone wants her syrup already," she called out loudly.

"Can't wait another minute for it. Like her mother."

"Oh, like her mother?" she rolled her eyes. "As if you haven't been circling the strawberry fields for the last two moons."

The other women laughed and filed into the village as she stayed to speak with her husband, who had a strange smirk on his face.

"What?"

He paused for a moment.

"The sun-heads are on their way to the village."

"NO!" she laughed loudly.

"They are!" he insisted with a smile. "The Delawares are bringing a Swedish embassy through the Conestoga lands to the Allegheny."

"Imagine that!" she said. "Never thought I'd get to see them with my own eyes. When?"

"This summer, I believe. And there is talk that the great sorceror from across the water is returning to the Mohawk."

"The black robe?"

"The same. But he will find no better reception than before."

"Let us hope he does not escape them again," she said sternly, "and find his way here."

"Perhaps they will be more careful," he added. "In any case, the Swedes do not appreciate his sorcery any better than the Mohawks. As long as they are here, *he* will not be."

"It is well," she agreed. "Now come, let us go to the feast."

A syrup of crushed strawberries, maple syrup, and water was ceremoniously brought to Gandeaktena and all the inhabitants of Gentaienton as they celebrated the return of this honored food source to the land. The day would be spent eating them fresh and drying them for later use, to be added corn bread and sagamité.

But when all was finished that night, Gandeaktena lay innocently in her father's lap in the main village plaza. Her mother leaned against his shoulder as they all stared into the village's central fire.

"Daddy?" she said.

"Yes?" he answered somewhat distractedly.

"When will I have a baby?"

"What?!" her mother sat up. "Child!"

Her father laughed.

"You have many years yet, little one. Why do you ask?"

She looked off in the distance and didn't seem overly concerned with answering.

"You will have many—*when it is time*," her mother declared pointedly.

"But why do some women not have any babies?"

Her mother looked imploringly at her husband.

"Every woman," he explained, "has within her a string of children, and on that string are as many as she is permitted to bring forth from the spirit world. Their faces are turned this way from beneath the ground, and if they are not enticed back into the spirit world, then they will be born and remain on the boards until they are able to crawl on the ground."

"How many children are on my string?"

"That," he said, "I do not know. Only the spirits know."

She seemed unsatisfied with that answer.

"But I *believe*, dear one, that you shall have many, many, *many* children. More, I think, than any other girl in the whole Erie nation. And your children will love you with great devotion, and carry your name in their hearts when you at last join your mother and I in the sky world. And everyone will say to us—what a great daughter you have raised, to be such a mother to so many!!"

Gandeaktena laughed aloud, her eyes beaming. Her mother shook her head at his tall tale, though also disguising the barest hint of a smile.

"Alright, now stop it! You will turn her into another Jigonhsaseh before too long!"

"And why not?!" he laughed, as he lifted his daughter playfully into the air. "A Great Peacemaker will come to the Erie and we will begin our own Confederacy! In the home of the great Gandeaktena, the Mother of Nations!"

She laughed right along with him, and when she finally went to bed that night, she fell asleep to the sweet echo of her dear father's words.

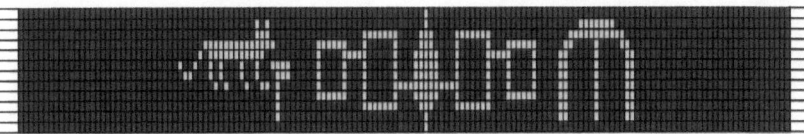

THE CATS AT WAR

Six years later, Gandeaktena was at the threshold of young womanhood. But it was now a very different world. The Five Nations of the Iroquois Confederacy, to the horror of all those who had learned to fear them, had invaded and completely shattered the Huron country, sending the remnants of that nation fleeing to other tribes and bringing home thousands of captives to burn or to naturalize and adopt. Without pause or mercy the Confederacy moved the next year against the Neutral Nation at the north end of Lake Erie, first sacking a village and then invading their entire homeland to the "complete ruin and desolation of the Neutral nation." Smaller nations also fell to Iroquois tomahawks, until only the Erie remained.

Now swelled with refugees from these shattered peoples, the Erie had a fierce fighting reputation that distinguished them from the mostly agricultural Hurons. And unlike the Hurons, they had kept clear of the French missionaries and traders, whom the Iroquois despised. They were moreover at peace with the westernmost and most populous branch of the Iroquois, the Seneca.

So while there had been general unease throughout the Northeastern forests, there was also some hope that the worst was now over.

But, by the spring of 1653, the Erie had opened a war against the Conestogas, their former trading partners with the colony of New Sweden. Great parties of men trooped off to meet the enemy in pitched battles, and the boys who were too young to participate formed little bands and skulked through the forest thirsting for blood, seldom accomplishing much but gaining stories and exploits to share with their countrymen at home.

One of these bands somehow came home bearing four young Conestoga captives, and they began whooping and hollering as they approached the village.

Gandeaktena ran out of her longhouse with some of her young relatives, and followed the crowd to the gate. Most everyone had a weapon in hand, from sticks to gunstock warclubs and tomahawks.

As the Eries lined up in facing ranks, the Conestoga youth were untied and shoved into the middle of the line. Blows and cuts rained down on them from every direction, as they staggered through them toward the village plaza.

This scene was nothing she hadn't witnessed before—but these four young men were not the usual proud warriors who prided themselves on enduring their suffering manfully and with spitting contempt for their tortures. They were hardly more than boys—a sorry group of youth whose bravado had got them caught up in something far more grim than they ever realized. They had gone off to war to win an easy honor— never truly understanding, as their elders did, what hatred awaited them if they failed.

There was a vicious look in the eyes of her loved ones and her young friends, as they struck them with clubs, drew daggers over their explosed flesh, and burned their fingers in pipe bowls. The youngest of them began to weep in the most unmanly way and was roundly jeered for it.

But Gandeaktena was moved with compassion and began to shake. The young Conestoga boys ended the gauntlet battered and squinting away the blood that poured over their barely distinguishable faces. The Erie boys grabbed them, and dragged them to the stakes to slowly burn them to death.

She could watch no more. She shook her head against the sight, and turned away, retiring to her longhouse with a great wound in her soul. But she would not be able to put the scene from her mind.

The blackness of night did not cloak the scenes from her memory, and the piteous screams of the youngest one continued to chill her blood until the first rays of dawn finally alighted on Gentaienton and the poor wretched creature was finally put out of his misery and his soul chased from the plaza.

From that day forward, Gandeaktena modestly remained in the background whenever captives were brought back to the village.

Not too long afterward, as she was carefully placing a hot rock from the fireplace into the kettle to warm up their evening soup, Gandeaktena greeted her father, who had returned from an emergency council meeting with worry on his face.

"So?" her mother asked anxiously. "What happened?"

"The peace with the Iroquois is shattered," he began somberly. "One of our men killed a Seneca by accident. They butchered almost our entire peace embassy in retaliation. Only five escaped alive."

His wife's hand went to her mouth as a cold sensation ran through her blood.

"All the elders are on fire. There will be war with the Seneca."

"Can we afford a second war?"

"No," he said gravely. "We cannot. For the time being we must put aside our emnity with the Conestogas."

"And what will Onondaga do?" she asked. Onondaga was the central fire or capital of the Iroquois confederacy.

"Hah!" he exclaimed with a frustrated shrug. "That we do not know. If Onondaga covers the fire, and the League stays away from the Western Door, then we shall only contend with the Seneca. If the League enters the war we shall contend with all the Five Nations at once."

"But will the fire be covered?"

"I do not know. The eastern Iroquois are in arms against the French. If they remain so occupied, they will not be anxious to bother us."

His wife shook her head. "Let's hope so."

She was silent for a few moments.

"Maybe the young men will trade some skirmishes with the Seneca and we can stay out of it until things become normal again. We are too strong a nation for them to overthrow entirely."

She looked up at her husband's face for reassurance, but she didn't like what she saw.

"It's almost time for dinner," she hurriedly changed the subject. "Gandeaktena—draw some water for your father."

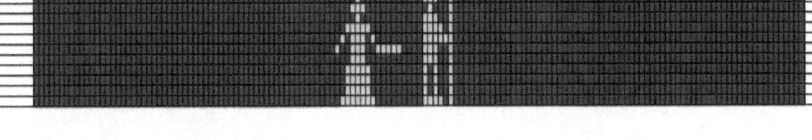

A GREAT CAPTAIN
OF THE CENTRAL FIRE

Later that year in the cool of September, Gandeaktena, her mother, and three of her friends were collecting firewood, when a joyous and fierce cry of victory sounded from the depth of the wood. A cold shudder ran through the girl's body, but her friends quickly turned to the source of the commotion. Their eyes wide with excitement, they hurried toward the town with half-finished bundles, nervously laughing and chattering among themselves.

Gandeaktena grew flush and silently stared at the ground. A couple more sticks lay before her on the forest floor, but she made no motion to pick them up. A few yards away, her mother noted the look of consternation on her daughter's face and shook her head.

In the distance, whoops of joy exploded from the town as drums began beating and the melody of a victory song floated out above the palisades.

Within the hour a small party of young warriors halloed out of the woods and approached with a bound, half-naked captive. A wild cheer rose among the assembled Erie, the news having already reached them of this prize that was being brought back to Gentaienton.

Six young Huron skirmishers had dared to sneak into the heart of Iroquoia itself to seize a great Captain of the Iroquois and return him alive.

The captive's face was hard and stern. He was quite a bit

older than all of his captors—and his grave and solemn demeanor only made their youthful taunts and swaggers seem hollow.

He was shoved into the gate, and the Erie women and children made sport of him for a time, hitting him with cudgels, crushing his fingers in their teeth, and burning him with lit firebrands as a prelude to what promised to be even greater punishment.

When the women and children had at last exhausted themselves in this cruel sport, the young men seized the Onondaga captain, dragged him into the largest longhouse in the town, and sat him down on the floor before the *oyander*, the male elders.

"My uncle," began the chief elder in a mocking though nervous tone, "it is well that the great Annenraes is here among his nephews at Gentaienton."

"Indeed," Annenraes replied in kind. "Your young men came to the very gates of Onondaga to win this prize."

"And you see how well beloved your name is among us—our longhouses were emptied for the number of those who came to caress you at our gates."

"It is so."

The Erie chief paused. There was something about Annenraes that unnerved him. Though bruised and beaten, the captive man did not show the false arrogance and frightened eyes of a common prisoner. There was a thoroughly stern and defiant look about the Onondaga—as if he was almost daring his captors to burn him.

The chief studied the fierce young men who had brought this upon him. *Fools. Barely weaned warriors who know nothing of war—who seek their own glory but leave everyone else to deal with the consequences. They'll have the whole League come down upon us for their stupidity.*

He would have to risk their annoyance.

"But we were not at war with Annenraes or the Great Fire. The Erie have enmity only for the Seneca."

Annenraes paused a moment, noting that the Huron youths now traded angry glances. He then responded gravely.

"Eighty of the finest warriors of Onondaga were cut down by your armies on their way home with spoils and captives from the great lake of the Hurons. Their blood cries from the ground, and their widows are mad with grief and thirsting for the blood of the Cats. Thus far we have let alone, my nephew, your castles which shelter the Hurons and the Tionontati and the Neutrals—this even though our enmity for those peoples causes us to pursue them even to the ends of earth. But who will cover the graves of the eighty? Who will restore the sun in the sky?

"My nephew, if you have ears to listen to the words of a slave and a captive, listen now to mine. For I am now nothing but a doomed man in your midst, and I may be on my journey to the spirit land before the next dawn rises on Gentaguenton. But I am a great warrior among my people, and one whose word is followed there as the river follows its bed.

"Until now we have covered the fire at Onondaga. The Seneca at our Western Door have waged war against the Cats, but the League has had no part of it. Annenraes has no fear to overthrow great nations. He has toppled the Hurons from their seats. He has scattered the Tionontati to the wind. And he has destroyed utterly the power of the Neutrals and the Atrakwae.

"But our people groan with war. We are not so numerous as our brothers whom you kill and devour without mercy. We have lost many sons and fathers, and if we had not taken the vanquished Hurons into our castle, there should be few men left to hunt deer in the forest or to fell the trees for our long-houses. The Hurons are as the brothers of the Onondaga now, as they are your brothers as well. And it is not right that they who share brothers should hate one another."

He paused for a moment, and encouraged by the softening faces of his captors, he pressed home his point.

"The Captain of the Iroquois has no fear of death. He would gladly be burned and eaten by his enemies. He would gladly strike terror into their hearts by standing unflinchingly at the height of his torments, singing his death song and calling upon the armies of his people to avenge him and extirpate the Nation of Cats from the earth.

"But there is no need for you to bring this fate upon your people. Your uncle Annenraes is before you alive, and he does not begrudge his nephews a little sport on his behalf, if you free him for the good of your nation, your wives, and your children.

"Release me now as a brother whom you have restored to life. And then, we shall journey together to Onondaga and conclude a peace with all the elders of the League, and we shall importune even the Seneca at our Western Door to cover their dead and speak no more of vengeance against the Nation of the Cats."

The Erie chief cast his eyes around the longhouse. His fellow elders and the *agoiander*, the noblewomen, nodded in admiration. Only the young Huron skirmishers sat with brows furrowed and smoldering eyes.

The Erie chief looked at them for a long time.

"Be of good cheer, my uncle," he spoke to Annenraes at last. "Your words from the heart do not lie, and the Erie are not thirsty for the blood of the Onondaga or eager for the destruction of the great fire. Let us feast now, that we have a great captain of the Onondaga among us. Annenraes was dead, and now he is restored to life."

As the assembled Erie loudly sounded their approval with shouts of "Ho! Ho!", the chief waved his wife to come to his side and spoke in her ear. As the commotion died down, she left his side and exited the longhouse, while the six skirmishers angrily sulked in the background.

"My uncle," said the Erie chief to Annenraes. "Listen to your nephew now. Our nation still grieves over the wound that was dealt us by your allies the Seneca, when our peace embassy of 30 strong, the heart of our nation, was cut down in their castle by an act of sheer treachery. There is one among us, a great *agoiander* and sister of one of the murdered ambassadors, who is still mad with grief. She has no more brother upon the earth. You, great warrior chief, will take his place and restore to her what she had lost. She is away, and we await her shortly.

"In the meantime, mothers, let us go out, and let a feast be opened! Let the Onondaga see what it is to come to the Nation of the Cats as a brother and not as an enemy!"

As the matriarchs brought out food and bowls for the feast, a crush of lively and beautiful young ladies laughed and tussled among themselves, playing with the necklaces and cannel coal pendants above their breasts as they draped fine garments and wampum on the great Onondaga captain.

At length the sister of the murdered ambassador returned to the village. She was an *agoiander*, a clan mother and respected member of the women's council of elders. But she did not, as expected, immediately present herself at the feast. So instead, the elders went to meet her at her cabin. The Erie chief smiled as he entered, and took her by the hand.

"Come, sister, dry your tears and be at peace. For your dead brother is restored to life. Your longhouse is once again whole. Prepare to regale your brother well, to give to him everything in your cabin that is his, and then to give him a gracious dismissal as we return him to the Great Fire at Onondaga."

She, however, began to weep.

"I will never dry my tears until my brother's death is avenged."

The chief stood in stunned silence as the strains of joyful music continued outside. The other elders' faces turned ashen.

"Sister," one of them said softly, sitting down before her, "consider the gravity of your demand. This is no ordinary brave, but a great captain from the Onondaga, from the great fire of all the Iroquois nations. This is an heir of Deganawida himself whom we have given to you—there are none more worthy to restore your brother to our nation. To turn this man from your longhouse will bring the entire Confederacy down upon our heads. We beg of you, sister, we beg of you for the good of the nation, to raise up this man and accept him as recompense for your loss."

She glared at him fiercely.

"The shade of my brother must be avenged."

⊞⊞⊞ ✝ ⊞⊞⊞

"**D**aughter," Gandeaktena's mother said, leaning into their family apartment in the longhouse. "Annenraes has been spared. A feast has been made ready. Come!"

The girl nodded in relief, rose from her seat upon the bed, and followed her mother toward the crowded main plaza, where her father and those of her clan were cheerfully feasting.

From the edge of the plaza, Gandeaktena saw Annenraes richly dressed and seated in a crowd of her older friends, joking with him and feeding him strips of meat. Others sang and shuffled in a round dance to the beat of the drum, and the less modest among them threw suggestive glances his way. He returned to all of them a knowing smile.

"He has a noble look," Gandeaktena's father observed. "If he advocates for us in the Councils of the League then I daresay we have little to fear."

"Mmm," nodded her uncle sagely.

"Gandeaktena!" called one of her friends from the square, motioning for her to come and join the crowd around the great Iroquois captain.

Gandeaktena bit her lip, though, and shook her head.

"Come on!" her friend motioned again, this time with more determination.

The girl shrank back behind her parents. Her mother looked at her worriedly, sighing to herself. She looked up at Gandeaktena's father, but he seemed unconcerned at his daughter's behavior.

Suddenly Gandeaktena was bumped roughly from behind, and the six young Huron skirmishers strode furiously past her toward the guest. Annenraes looked up in puzzlement as they approached. His attending coterie of nubile Erie girls, the mirth now vanishing from their faces, began slinking away. Without a word, the young men lifted him from the ground and shoved him toward the cabin where the elders now sat.

The drums stopped abruptly, as if an evil spirit had blown wailing through the center of the town. Puzzled glances went back and forth among the assembled Eries outside as Annenraes was led inside the woman's cabin.

Gandeaktena saw him silhouetted against the interior fire while the six young men tore off his clothes and held him fast before his adoptive sister and the Erie elders.

Annenraes steeled his expression and lifted his chin.

"It is well," he declared defiantly, loud enough even for those outside to hear. "It is well. An entire people will be burned in my person, my death will be cruelly avenged, and the Cats will vanish from the earth." He began to sing a wild and proud song.

The six young Hurons then dragged him out of the cabin toward the platform and the stake, and their kinswoman, she who had sealed the Onondaga's fate, followed closely behind, a look of pure hatred upon her face.

Gandeaktena and her mother turned in grim sadness toward their longhouse, and the girl's final image of the scene—which she never forgot all of her days—was of the chief of Gentaienton burying his head in his hands.

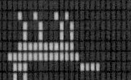

DIES ERIE

August, 1654.

The morning wind blew peacefully over the waters of the Allegheny River, as the earliest rays of sun cast a dim light over its waves. Along its banks, a bobcat waddled down for a drink. Suddenly it paused. The symphony of birds had grown strangely quiet. Sniffing the air, the bobcat suddenly scampered away from the bank and into the brush, as a distant and strange rumble reverberated from the ground.

A trembling fugitive, half-dead from blood loss and exhaustion, tripped and stumbled her way toward the palisade of a sleeping Gentaienton. With her last ounce of strength she cried out in as loud a voice as she could muster—and though it came out little more than a coarse whisper, it was enough. The sentries ran out, seized her and whisked her into the palisade, where between gasps of pain and hysteria she choked out in half-sentences all that she had seen during the night.

Within half an hour, hundreds more bloody and exhausted souls poured out of the forests. They only stopped long enough to take their breath and confirm that the Iroquois had invaded with an army over a thousand strong, then they continued their panicked flight to the southeast toward Rigué.

Gandeaktena was startled awake to violent shaking. "Get up! Get up!"

Her mother's eyes darted with terror in the pre-dawn light.

"Iroquois! Get up!"

Gandeaktena sprung off her mat. Like all of her kin, she had nursed a dread of this very moment for the last several years—but now that it was upon her there was no time for self-pity. Her mother hurriedly filled a small basket with dried meat and cornmeal.

"Go find your father!", she yelled.

Gandeaktena ran from the apartment and out the door of the longhouse. When she got to the northern palisade she saw her father in animated discussion with the war chief and her male relatives, smearing themselves with paint and gripping knives, tomahawks, and ball-headed clubs. One brandished an arquebus and practiced sighting it toward the woods.

She started tentatively toward them, but as her father saw her approach, he shot her a stern look and, with a sharp motion of his head and hands, directed her back to their longhouse. She stood still for a moment, moved by some strange impulse to ignore the chaos about her and stare at him. When the haste finally reasserted itself in her mind, she darted back into her longhouse.

"*Where is your father?!*" her mother cried out.

"With the men on the palisade."

Mother turned away, nodding in resignation and wiping the corner of her eye.

"Here. Take this basket. We must leave."

"Do we wait for father?" Gandeaktena asked, though she had guessed the answer already.

"Father will stay," his mother replied stoically. "Father will stay."

Within minutes, the women and children of Gentaien-ton had started on the southwestern road to Rigué. They marched swiftly at a safe distance away from the river, continually squinting through the trees out at the water. The clan mothers talked in low tones amongst themselves.

Suddenly the women in the lead stopped.

Before them, strewn about the ground, lay five of their neighbors scalped and bathed in blood. The *agoiander* came forward to survey the grim scene, while the others looked at each other and shot worried glances around them and up the road ahead. The trees and the ground cover betrayed no evidence that a great army had passed this way—perhaps it was only an advance unit of Iroquois scouts.

"Push on, push on!" one of the *agoiander* demanded impetuously. But though everyone felt the same urgency, no one moved. Then one of the clan sisters called out and pointed to a beech tree, upon which the Iroquois had written a message in pictographs:

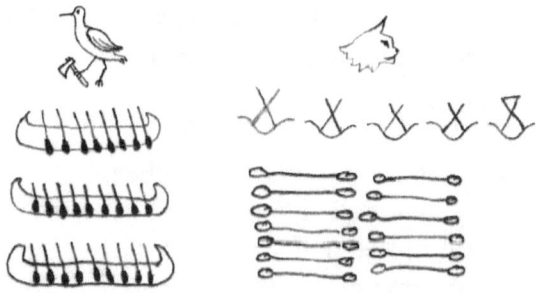

26 men of the Snipe clan to Rigué; 5 Erie killed, 13 taken prisoner

The *agoiander* fell deathly silent and looked back toward home. The Iroquois had cut them off.

Gentaienton fell within the hour. The Iroquois army that streamed out of the woods completely overwhelmed the men's defenses, chopping through the palisade with iron hatchets. They wrought carnage among those inhabitants still left within its walls before they fired the longhouses and started in separate bands toward the town of Rigué. Gandeaktena never saw her home, or her father, again.

The Erie women on the road were surprised by a party of Oneida, covered in blood. The Oneida ordered the women seated on the ground, bound their arms behind them, and then tied Gandeaktena, her mother, and her clan sisters together. After a short time, a warrior lifted them onto their feet and dragged them along the road.

⊞⊞⊞ ✝ ⊞⊞⊞

Gandeaktena pulled back on her bound hands and flinched instinctively as a small group of Iroquois scouts smeared in paint came out of the woods next to her. One of the scouts, wearing around his neck the same kind of black pendant her countrymen wore, glared at her briefly before he approached the war captain who had held them prisoner, an Oneida named Atondatochan.

"Kwe!" the scout shouted boldly.

"What news?" replied Atondatochan.

"Rigué is abandoned," the scout answered. His dialect was more intelligible than the swallowed consonants of Seneca. "The Cats have all taken flight and their trail leads south along the Venango toward the Ohio. Only the sick and old remain."

"Hm," he nodded. "Have the League's chiefs arrived?"

"We are there alone."

Atondatochan looked out in the direction of the river.

No stomach for war, these Erie. They'll sneak even to the gates of Onondaga for a scalp and play the brave very well when they outnumber you. But march an army into their country and they leave their grandfathers and their invalids to defend it.

"We are to meet at Rigué, so we shall join you there and await the Onondaga. We will have time to ready our prisoners before then."

Gandeaktena turned nervously toward her mother, but her mother stared straight ahead.

"It is well," replied the scout. "When you have secured the town we will follow the trail of the Riguehronnons into the mountains. We will keep Ochionagueras informed."

Atondatochan nodded. As the scouting party glided back into the woods toward Rigué, arquebuses in hand, he looked over his captives and then his own men.

Our losses have been thankfully minimal so far. Hopefully that will keep these men out of mischief. If I can persuade them to not make sport of the captives, so much the better. We are not the Seneca that we can afford to lose dozens in war and then sacrifice all our captives.

He eyed Gandeaktena. *My daughter's age, this one; and she has a modest and humble face.*

"Do you fear being burnt?" he called to her.

She shot a worried glance over toward her mother, whose face was as stone.

The Iroquois continued staring at her, so not knowing what else to do, she nodded.

The warrior looked at her, then her mother, and suddenly laughed.

"Be of good cheer," he reassured them with a smile. "You are under the protection of Atondatochan."

Atondatochan led his captives through the palisade of Rigué, now full of Iroquois. He marched them toward the main plaza across from the scaffold on which the Riguehronnon tortured their prisoners. An icy chill of death passed through each of the women.

"Sit," he gestured, and walked off toward the largest longhouse.

A few of his younger warriors broke away to investigate the abandoned town, joking with the band of scouts who had already begun throwing beaver pelts and other loot into the plaza. But the veterans sat upon the ground with their captives, apparently more interested in rest than plunder. Gandeaktena fervently prayed to Tharonhiawagon, the Sky Holder, for the delivery of her kin.

Soon a great din came out of the forest, as a few hundred more Iroquois approached the palisade of Rigué. From the scaffold along the palisade, some of the young Oneida began to shout:

"Aharihon! Aharihon!"

The name electrified the young men at the palisades, who poured out to see this famed warrior of the Onondaga flush with victory. Gandeaktena looked over at Atondatochan, who seemed to have a look of disgust on his face. He called his lieutenant over, said something in his ear very emphatically, then spat on the ground, turned, and left the plaza.

Aharihon entered Rigué with about 40 Erie captives before him. He marched them to the plaza and flung them down upon the ground. Then he glared at the women for a long time; Gandeaktena shut her eyes.

"Whose captives are these?" he demanded imperiously.

"They are under the mantle of Atondatochan," replied the lieutenant.

"Then bring out Atondatochan," Aharihon demanded. "For my brother lies fallen at Gentaienton, and his shade demands to see the blood of the Cats spilled this very hour."

"Thou hast thine own captives," the Oneida shot back. "And there is the stake."

"These are dogs," Aharihon scowled. "Forty even is not enough to appease the shade of my brother, for of these not a one is worthy to take his place. I am taking them to Onondaga, where my kin shall be generous with their welcomes and caresses, and welcome them in the houses of the Iroquois."

At that moment Atondatochan returned, and glared at Aharihon.

"These women, they are mine. Let the Onondaga attend to his own."

Aharihon glared at him defiantly, but in the end he had to content himself with a fresh group of prisoners brought in by the remainder of the Onondaga army.

Those unfortunates were bludgeoned, bitten, carved with knives and mutilated before being forced to ascend the scaffold and endure a long night of unspeakable torture at the hands of the Iroquois. Gandeaktena and the women had been spared. However, many times within those horrible hours, during which they dared neither to sleep nor to utter a sound, she thought that a hatchet blow to the head would be vastly preferable to the soul-shattering anguish of watching her kin scream and writhe in the flames.

The next morning, the cruel game having spent itself out and the last mutilated victims dispatched in sacrifice to the war spirit Agreskoue and the dawning sun, the Iroquois army quit Rigué with their captives and set the town to the torch. Black smoke billowed into the sky as the army pushed its captives south in pursuit of remaining Erie.

For five days they tracked the fugitives through the woods. At last, the Riguehronnons repented of their flight and, having learned that the number of Iroquois warriors was far smaller than their own, resolved to make a final stand. Within a few short hours, a strong palisade of newly hewn tree trunks had been thrown up, the women and children were secured within the makeshift fort, and the remaining warriors of the Erie nation trained their eyes on the surrounding wood and awaited the enemy.

MASTERS OF LIFE
AND DEATH

With over a thousand men behind him, the young war captain of all the Iroquois, Jean Baptiste Ochionaguer-as, surveyed the bristling palisades before him.

A few weeks before he had set out from Onondaga, he had learned of the Christian mysteries from Father Simon Le Moyne, a Black Robe who had come from Quebec to broker peace with the Great Fire at Onondaga. As the time drew nigh for the warriors to take the field and the Black Robe to return to Quebec, the Captain asked him for Baptism. But the priest demurred, instructing Ochionagueras to be patient, and to wait for some future journey to be finally counted among the faithful.

"How now, my brother?" the Captain replied. "If from this day forth I possess the Faith, cannot I be a Christian? Have you power over death to forbid its attacking me without orders from you? Will our enemies' arrows become blunted for my sake? Do you wish me, at each step that I take in battle, to fear hell more than death? Unless you baptize me, I shall be without courage, and shall not dare to face the conflict. Baptize me, for I am determined to obey you—and I give you my word that I will live and die as a Christian."

Moved by the warrior's piety, Father Le Moyne washed him early the next morning in the waters of regeneration, the first Iroquois to be baptized in the state of health, and christened him Jean Baptiste.

The Captain embraced the Father.

"Henceforth," he said, "Jesus will be my only hope and my all."

⌶ ⌶ ⌶

Dressed to intimidate the Erie in the attire of Frenchmen, Jean Baptiste and Aharihon together approached the hastily raised fort.

Above the palisade appeared the great war chief of the Erie, who raised his head, looked down his nose, and scowled.

"Your arms stretch too far, Iroquois, over the Nation of the Cats! Turn them elsewhere, before we cut them from your shoulders and boil them in the kettle."

"Listen to me now," replied Jean Baptiste. "Did you think even now that you could escape justice? You have made war upon our Western Door and barbarously murdered a peace embassy. You have cut down the armies of the Central Fire when the sun was in the sky and we were at peace. You have come to our very gates to seize and burn the Onondagas and eat the heads of our nation. All the Five Nations are on fire at your treachery.

"And yet, though the blood of our kin cries from the ground, though the sun is dark in the sky, the wrath of the Iroquois toward the Cats is yet able to be appeased. As the Master of Life showed mercy even toward his enemies, so I too show mercy to you. Surrender, make satisfaction, and even now thy people will be suffered to return to thy homeland. But if you refuse our entreaties and fail to give consolation for your crimes against the League, be assured of this: your Nation will be destroyed utterly and extirpated from the face of the earth."

Interpreting this unusual declaration of mercy as a sign of weakness, the Erie chief and his generals all laughed aloud.

"The Nation of the Cat numbers twice as many warriors as the whole League. And our palisade is proof against your arms. We have no need for your mercy."

Jean Baptiste smirked.

"To your nation and to our nations alike the shattered Hurons have carried the words of He Who Has Made All. But while we Iroquois have invited the Black Robes to our castles, you Erie remain without sense and without the Prayer that gives life. For he is wise who fears neither the firebrands of the enemy, which burn only for a little while, but only the flames of hell which burn forever."

The Erie chief laughed.

"Who are these Black Robes? Bring them out, so that I might see who fights for you."

"It is the Master of Life who fights for us," replied Jean Baptiste. "You will be ruined if you resist Him."

"Who is this Master of Life?" the Erie demanded with a contemptuous sneer. "We acknowledge none but our arms and hatchets." His warriors all laughed boisterously.

Jean Baptiste nodded gravely and signaled behind him. The Iroquois camp exploded with a terrible war-cry and its warriors rushed the palisades from all sides.

The Erie answered them with a murderous flood of arrows and shot, and the first wave of Iroquois attackers dropped lifeless to the ground. Undaunted, their fellow warriors continued to press on toward the fort, dashing as quickly as they could out of the forests and toward the palisades. But they too were cut down by the musket shot pouring out of the fort, which fell as steady as a deadly rain.

The sight of so many of their warriors falling inflamed the Iroquois to avenge their losses on their enemy, but each and every charge of the fort ended in doom. Again and again, every which way, the Iroquois drove forward, but no matter which great captain led the charge, he ended up pierced and bloody beneath the walls, his soul awaiting its flight toward the west. The Eries laughed and continued to taunt the Iroquois: "Who

is this Master of Life?! Where are his arquebuses? Where are
his hatchets?"

Jean Baptiste shook his head. *We shall never take them this
way. Jesus, have pity on us.*

Another assault was being readied but he waved it off. A
great cheer went up from the Erie at the mighty Iroquois being humbled at last, and the hearts of the Onondaga captains
burned in fury.

Jean Baptiste had scored resounding successes in the Erie
country through surprise, and his ferocious attacks had put
to flight a much greater army. But now the Erie army was
trapped, cornered, and turned to face its attacker...and with
nothing to lose, they had finally found the courage to stand
their ground.

Master of Life, he murmured, *Ochionaguaras does not fear
to die or be burned by his enemies. But Thou who has sent Thy
black robes to the country of the Onondaga, Thou who hast at last
set the sun of peace in the sky between the Iroquois and the French
and brought the waters of Baptism to the Iroquois, see that these
infidels who hate Thy name do not triumph.*

He made the sign of the cross, studied the battlements of
the fort then looked over at his men, whose demoralized faces
already betrayed their ebbing morale.

Suddenly, Jean Baptiste shot a glance back toward the
river, his eyes full of purpose. Then he turned around to see
Atondatochan toward the rear of the army.

"Bring Atondatochan!" he ordered a young brave.

As soon as the Oneida captain arrived, Jean Baptiste pulled
him in.

"Send men to the river. Have them bring here every canoe
they can carry."

Atondatochan nodded and ran to fulfill his commission. If
the request puzzled him, he didn't show it.

Well behind the Iroquois lines, far enough from the palisade walls to be out of danger, Gandeaktena, her mother, and countless other Erie prisoners sat upon the ground, their bonds fixed to the earth by stout stakes.

A few of the Iroquois men had stayed behind to guard the captives, but there was also a large group of women busying themselves around the Iroquois camp. These were enslaved captives from a number of conquered nations—the Hurons, Tionontati, Neutrals, and the Adirondacks, the Algonquian nations to the north and the west.

These women had been drafted into service as the cooks and the supply train of the Iroquois army, gathering whatever they could from the forest around them and dutifully preparing whatever game the warriors laid at their feet. They saw to their responsibilities conscientiously and as carefully if they had been free Iroquois women. For anyone among them who shirked their duties or proved a hindrance to the fighting men of the League in an enemy land was rewarded with a swift hatchet blow to the skull.

One of these captives caught Gandeaktena's attention. She was middle aged and had two twins roughly the same age as Gandeaktena herself, who followed her as she made rounds among the prisoners. She traded some kind words of encouragement with everyone, but every once in a while she would stop with tears in her eyes and embrace a Huron captive with the warmth and love of old friendship. Gandeaktena surmised that she must have been of that shattered nation as well.

Eventually the Huron captive came to Gandeaktena and her mother, her eyes filled with compassion. She sat down and offered the prisoners a bit of mush.

"Kwe. Eat well and regain your strength," she said.

"Will they spare us?" Gandeaktena's mother asked very frankly.

"I do not know," the Huron replied. "In truth, I do not know if they will even spare me. For I am old and these knees are ravaged with disease. But I will pray to He who has Made All, that whatever his adorable will be for poor Martha, that he have pity on you his daughters of the Cat Nation and bring them safely to Onondaga."

"But do you not fear to die?" Gandeaktena's mother asked somewhat skeptically. "Why do you pray that he spare us and not you as well?"

She smiled in kindness.

"I have nothing on Earth save my sons. And even they can be taken from me in a moment. But I will have everything in heaven and enjoy it forever; and they too, whom my brother gave the life of Baptism before we left Onondaga, are destined for nothing but happiness. What, then, should poor Martha fear from death? But ah, how I would pity your deaths a thousand times more!"

"You mock me, Huron," her mother replied curtly. "How do you pity the death of an enemy above your own?"

"Have the Hurons who lived among you not yet opened the eyes of the Cats? For if you and your daughter perished today, you would perish as infidels and without consolation of the life eternal that awaits the baptized."

"We had," said Gandeaktena's mother sharply, "an old Huron among us who was of the Prayer and who led the prayers among your countrymen. But his teaching drew only scorn, and none of our elders gave him any heed."

"Ahh," nodded Martha. "it was just so in our country for many years. I remember well how the good Joseph Chiwatenhwa and his family were alone in prayer amidst a sea of doubters and scoffers. But the misfortunes of plague and war that befell our nation turned the minds of many. Contarea that openly mocked God was the first to be destroyed by the Iroquois, and through calamity His adorable will saw to it that hearts of the Hurons were softened and brought to the waters of Baptism."

"Was it also His will that you be destroyed?" the Erie replied sarcastically.

"Of course! Who can deny it?" Martha replied. "It was indeed His will that the fires of the Iroquois consumed our country and scattered us like birds across the lands. Do not judge, though, the poor Hurons only by our losses. We who had Baptism endured in spirit, though we were beaten and bound and dragged to the very castles of enemies and infidels. For whatever our bodies endured, our souls remained saved by those waters, and we counted ourselves worthy to suffer for Christ Jesus as He had for us."

She fell silent, as if lost in a devotional reverie.

"How..." piped up Gandeaktena impulsively, her modesty for once overcome by her curiosity. But her mother glared at her, so she grew flush and fell silent.

"No, child," said Martha. "You do no wrong. Ask your question of me."

"How....is one baptized?"

Martha looked at the girl and studied her face, as a tear came from the corner of her eye.

"Child, it is not a thing lightly done. The Black Robes baptize only those who prove themselves worthy. But even so, one may be baptized if one is in the perils of death. My brother"—and here she choked a little—"my brother Tsondihwane did this very thing with many of our children at Onondaga. But he fell at Rigué and now, I pray, enjoys the bliss of paradise."

She touched her hand to her forehead, breast, and shoulders; a gesture that Gandeaktena had seen other Hurons make.

"Beautiful child," Martha said, "you have a modest and brave countenance. Be strong, and pray to Him who has Made All, and you will see how it will strengthen you for all that He wills you to endure." She called her young sons to her side and then moved on to the other captives with a slight limp.

Gandeaktena watched her serene face as long as she could, and then turned her thoughts to wondering about that mysterious and distant Spirit who thought the universe into being.

Rivers were the highways of the Eastern Woodlands, used whenever possible for everything from trade to war parties. The Iroquois knew every portage for connecting one river system to another. During a long journey, when the boats were no longer needed and the travelers were compelled to proceed on foot, they weighted their canoes down with stones and sunk them to the bottom of the river for later retrieval.

However, the Iroquois had not the canoe-craft as the Adirondacks or Algonquins. The lands of the latter were blessed with abundant quantities of the paper birch, whose bark could be peeled in one great sheet off a tree. The Algonquin birchbark canoe was a mastery of design: light and easy to carry, fleet in the water, and beautiful besides. But its thin, light coating of birchbark was easily torn, and the black robes who regularly traveled in it wryly and truthfully observed in their letters back home that they were only a few sheets of paper away from drowning.

Since the Iroquois had no suitable paper birch in their country, they made their canoes of thick, rough elm bark, peeled off the tree, folded in half, and sewn up the bow and stern. Their elm bark canoes were bulky, slow, and heavy. But all of those disadvantages they had in the water were now about to prove an invaluable asset on the field of battle.

Bearing their heavy canoes in front of them like great shields, the Iroquois army advanced one more time on the Erie fort. This time, the arrows and many of the arquebus balls either lodged into or bounced harmlessly off the dense canoe hulls. In a state of alarm, the Erie warriors redoubled their efforts, trying to seek out any exposed flesh—but though they managed to fell some of the more incautious Iroquois, a great many of the enemy safely reached the walls of the fort. And now the Eries' limited supply of powder and shot had been exhausted; no more arquebus fire was heard from the fort.

Holding their canoes above them for protection, the Iroquois began to chop at the walls with their iron hatchets. But the Erie had built well, so the going was slow. Then a group of bold Iroquois warriors suddenly flipped their canoe and leaned it against the palisade—exposing themselves to enemy arrows but then, to the utter astonishment of the Erie, clambering up the canoe to the top of the wall. The first Iroquois warrior atop the palisade gave a great yell of victory before he was cut down, but in his bold act of daring bravery, he had exposed a weakness in the enemy's defense.

Jean Baptiste signaled the men still away from the walls to lay down a short burst of covering fire and approach. The Erie huddled down behind the palisade to protect themselves, and in those few moments, the Iroquois besiegers propped their canoes against the wall, scaled them like ladders to the top of the palisades, and fell down upon the Erie with fury. Those Iroquois who had kept up the suppressing fire now rushed in to give them aid.

Astounded at the boldness of the Iroquois and at their sudden reversal of fortune, the Erie warriors inside the fort were thrown into chaos. As the Iroquois streamed in from the top of the palisade and cut down the defending force in hand-to-hand combat, the panicked Erie began to stream out of the makeshift gate toward the woods. Many of them were slain as soon as they left the protection of the fort, and those who managed to escape that first gauntlet ran right into the Onondaga, whose hatchets and war clubs tore through the fleeing Erie and into the open gate.

Inside, as it was recounted later to the Jesuit chroniclers, the Onondaga "wrought such carnage among the women and children, that the blood was knee-deep in certain places."

The great and proud Erie nation found its trust in arms and hatchets fatally misplaced. It never recovered from the invasion, and the people of Gentaienton as a distinct group were never heard from again in the annals of history. Surviving remnants of the nation fled far to the south to Virginia, whose colonists marveled at and feared this strange and fierce band of "Rickohokans," northern Indians who appeared out of nowhere from the mountains and made war upon the local tribes. Fleeing further still to the Carolinas, the Erie remnants became known to the surrounding nations as the Westo—"the enemy". There they raided hostile and friendly tribes alike to supply an insidious traffic in human beings, until they were utterly defeated by the Shawnee in 1680 and auctioned off in the infamous slave market they had once fed.

For their part, the blood-soaked Iroquois who now stood amidst the ruins of the Erie fort had more than avenged the shade of Annenraes. But that victory came at a heavy cost, and the League's armies spent a full two months in the enemy's country burying their dead.

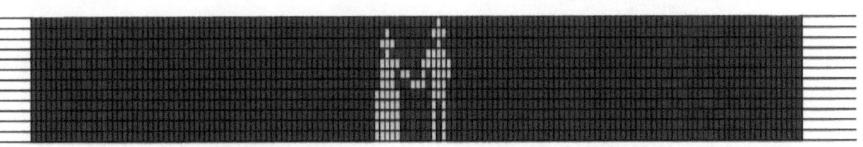

JOURNEY TO THE STANDING STONE

"**U**p!" directed the Oneida curtly as he pulled up the stakes holding Gandeaktena and her mother fast to the ground. With difficulty she raised herself, then aided her mother.

The women in the charge of Atondatochan had not been treated badly thus far in their journey to Iroquoia—but what they had already seen and what they feared upon arrival in the enemy's village consumed their minds far beyond their immediate comfort. The crushing, debilitating fear of being captured and led away by the enemy was something that all shared in that brutal time of perpetual war. It weighed on Gandeaktena's soul quite enough when she had been out in the fields, or gathering firewood. But to wake from the land of dreams while tied to a stake in the ground and being dragged into the gates of those who utterly despised her—that was too much to bear for the young girl. And it was, perhaps, her own fear of such an end that had given her such an empathy for the poor souls who had once been brought in bonds to Gentaienton.

Overcome now, Gandeaktena began to weep, but her mother quickly gave her an assuring look and bade her with a motion of the head to dry her tears on her shoulder.

Atondatochan saw the exchange, and he walked over Gandeaktena.

"Young one," he said with a kind look. "it is unbecoming of a maiden to weep when she is under the mantle of the great Captain of the Oneida."

She nodded, her eyes downcast still. The other Erie women looked hopefully at Atondatochan for some indication of their fate.

"The insolence of your leaders has proved the downfall of your nation, but the platform and stake in that land have been burnt utterly, so that nothing remains of them to torment us. Did the castles of Sagochiendagehté not take in the Huron, and the Tionontati, and the Neutrals, when these nations begged mercy and protection from the sons of Deganawida?"

"Come now, be of good cheer," he said kindly and earnestly, though he knew his words were of little comfort. "The great Captain of the Oneida commands much respect in his homeland, and he will plead all your cases before the elders."

Gandeaktena nodded again gratefully, this time looking up into his eyes, which were kind and solemn. Perhaps she had no reason to trust him. But she did nonetheless.

⊞⊞⊞⊞ ✝ ⊞⊞⊞⊞

The Thunder Beings were in the sky along the road to Oneida, a soft rain falling through the forest on captive and captor alike as they marched. The Iroquois had a strangely calm air about them, but they also were keen to move swiftly, as some of the Riguehronnon had regrouped and were launching retaliatory attacks on the victorious army.

Gandeaktena found herself in a strange peace at times, until the fear and the memories came back and sat like a stone within her stomach.

As their captors took a rest around mid-day, Gandeaktena and her mother were forcibly seated next to a Huron warrior and a familiar woman huddled by the side of the road in earnest conversation, two young boys standing near them. It was Martha Aatio, the Huron whom they had met at Rigué.

She smiled, but there was suffering in that rain-soaked face.

"It gladdens my heart to see you both again."

"And we you," replied Gandeaktena's mother. She looked down. "Your knee?"

Martha shook her head. "It is worse each day. Soon I will not be able to walk."

The Erie looked grave and leaned in close, one mother to another. "And what of your sons?"

"There are many good Hurons at Onondaga," said the warrior beside her. "We will see to it that they are provided for."

"But Martha," he continued earnestly, "do not concern yourself with the things of this world. For you know that Oto-henha speaks truly when he says that he will look after her sons as his own."

"I know it," she replied through tears, "I know it. But I fear greatly what may befall them. If they forget their Baptism, and become no better than infidels and profligates..."

"And what," he replied, "is there poor Martha can do to prevent this, even if she remained with them all their days? He Who has Made All has given them wills as he has given you yours, and He would not that they perish. Besides, those who pray will stand guard over their souls and see that they do not turn to wickedness.

"But attend to your own soul now, Martha, for we all stand here in peril and without the consolations of the Black Robe to prepare us for death. Be strong. Keep your promise to God no matter what may befall you or your children, and die in the profession of the faith."

She nodded in humility at the rebuke. "You are right, Otohenha. You are right."

"Now come," Otohenha said. "Let us make haste."

Just then, however, an Onondaga warrior strode up to

them with a purposeful fire in his eyes. He made a direct path to the twins, who shrunk back in fear.

The Iroquois grabbed one of the boys, and threw him on his knees to the ground. He then seized the other and threw him next to his brother. Without pausing, he lifted his hatchet in the air and brained the first. The second son barely had time to steel himself for the blow before his skull too was split.

As their blood streamed across the rain-soaked soil, the Onondaga glared straight at their mother and sneered.

"These are dead dogs. There is nothing to be done but to cast them upon the dunghill."

He strode off without a further word.

Martha Aatio sat shocked and trembling, her hands in spasms for a few moments, as Otohenha picked her up from the ground.

"Come now Martha," he said anxiously.

She cried aloud as her weight pressed down on her knee, and she shuddered and made a face of excruciating pain.

"Oh my Jesus," she whimpered, still trembling. "O my Jesus, have pity on me."

As Otohenha helped Martha limp back to her place in the line, Gandeaktena's mother bit her lip in tears, reached over to her own daughter and cradled that innocent head in her shoulder as far as her bonds would allow.

Two days later, Gandeaktena and her mother passed upon the trail the partially burnt corpse of a woman. Martha Aatio had joined her sons in the Christian Heaven that she had so earnestly sought.

Night fell upon the path, and the prisoners were again staked to the ground. Unable to sleep under the moonlight that filtered in among the trees, Gandeaktena whispered, "I am very afraid, mother."

"I know child," she replied. She feared the worst as well, but more for her young daughter than herself.

"Listen to me, Gandeaktena," she began in a low tone, hoping that some stern direction would give her daughter something to focus on. "The Iroquois will look for any cause to put us both to death. You must not give them any reason to do so. Behave modestly, but do as you are told. Be prompt with your attention when asked and be retiring and meek at all other times. If the Iroquois ask you to dance, or to sing, you are to do so and not shrink away. You must, you *must* obey your new mistress in all things."

"I will," the girl nodded.

"Do not be insolent, do not shirk your duties, and do not refuse your participation in any amusements or the attention of those who befriend you. You are young, and if you prove yourself docile and obedient, they will have pity on you."

Gandeaktena looked imploringly into her mother's dark, moonlit eyes.

"And I will do the same," the latter concluded reassuringly.

She paused, and the crickets in the background were alone in their chirping for a moment.

"Will they let us live?"

"I do not know, daughter," she admitted. "But be brave and strong. If all hope is lost, then sing as long and as loud as you can, and show them how an Erie dies. And remember always, if the pain becomes too great for you, that the shade of your father awaits our embrace in the lands of the west."

She fell silent. A wolf howled in the distance.

The terrors of the night did not abate by the morning. The shivering Erie prisoners were led bound through crowds of jeering Oneida women who struck them in retaliatory rage for all the loved ones they, too, had lost during this war. The poor captives were herded into the enemy palisade, from which there was no hope of escape, and they were made to sing. Days they passed on the edge of death as the council of Oneida debated their fate.

In the end, thanks in part to the sage recommendations of Atondatochan, the *agoiander* of the Standing Stone agreed to adopt all the Erie captives. Henceforth, Gandeaktena and her mother would be Iroquois.

THE MOODY HURON

1665.

For ten years, Gandeaktena followed her mother's advice and served her Oneida captors most honorably. The life of an Iroquois slave, especially a young woman, was tenuous and liable to end in an instant if she tried to escape or raised the ire of her hosts. But the shy maiden from the Cat Nation never gave anyone cause for complaint, and she was generally treated kindly by those in her longhouse.

Under her Erie mother's ever-watchful eye, Gandeaktena's modesty and demure, unassuming manner won the hearts of her adopted Oneida family. She even made a few close friends, though when these adorned themselves to attract the attention of men, or swayed like tall corn in the woman dances, or went out of curiosity to participate in councils, she naturally demurred as much as she thought appropriate, replying: "It is more seemly for a slave to be retiring than to give herself up to enjoyments."

But if they persisted, then she would not be obstinate. She put on whatever garments and beads her friends and family bade her wear and amused herself, danced, and feasted in the manner expected of an Iroquois maiden.

One midday, as Gandeaktena and her aunt—for so did she now call the clan matriarch who had adopted her into her longhouse—ate before their fire in the center of longhouse, the old woman scooped some hickory milk into her ladle and looked with a twinkle in her eye at her adopted niece, who was petting the dog distractedly.

"Young one," she said, with a strange hint of mock seriousness. "It is time that you marry."

"Marry, aunt?"

"Indeed," she replied. "I am an old woman, and you will have need of a husband to bring you meat and to give you children."

Despite it having long been a dream of hers, Gandeaktena blushed.

"Come now, young one!" her aunt chided. "You are a child no longer. It is unseemly of you to keep to yourself."

"I am sorry, aunt," the girl replied.

"Do not be sorry—but listen to what I tell you."

"I will, aunt."

"Do you not know it is time for you now to marry? Dio you not want for a husband? And children?"

"I do."

"Then delay no longer! Be more free with yourself, and do not hide yourself from the view of the warriors. Your face is not unappealing, and you have a meek disposition. It will not be said of my niece that she would drive a husband from her longhouse with chattering."

Gandeaktena fell silent—more because of the compliment than the rebuke.

"Listen to me. Your aunt knows your disposition. She sees that you are a shy, retiring girl, and not one to parade yourself about the village or suffer suitors to visit your bed. But if such a man could be found that would overlook such a minor fault, you would do well to accept his offer at the first opportunity."

The matriarch's expression had been stern until now, but her eyes suddenly twinkled with barely concealed amusement. "What do you think of Tonsahoten?"

Gandeaktena shrugged. He was a Huron by birth but one of those naturalized captives who had gradually become more Iroquois than the Iroquois themselves. She had never thought of him as a husband certainly—although he was a fine man with a handsome face, he had a legendarily tempestuous disposition that did not endear him to those Oneida girls who only sought charming words and flattery. Also, in his former country he had been baptized into the Prayer of the black robes, which was a further mark against him.

Her aunt continued, "Few men would dare to claim themselves a better warrior than he. He commands great respect among the *agoiander*. And most of all, little one: he is quite fond of you."

Gandeaktena blushed again and stared at the ground as her aunt laughed.

"Go now," she waved toward the door and chuckled, "Gather more wood and then return quickly and make yourself ready. He will come and sup with us tonight."

The girl rose and, in her haste, stepped on the dog's tail, who yelped and ran away.

"Go! Go!" her aunt laughed uncontrollably, as the girl ran out the door.

That evening the esteemed young warrior Francis Xavier Tonsahoten arrived at the longhouse of Gandeaktena's aunt and paid his respects to all present. He took his place before the fire stoically, making every effort not to alight his eyes too intently on the young woman he was there to see. For her part, Gandeaktena served him his meat graciously, if somewhat dispassionately, and the young man relished every chance he had to nod to her in thanks for a pleasantry. In such fashion, they passed the meal, and as they all relaxed before the central fire, the matriarch's tone became suddenly more serious.

"It is well, esteemed warrior, that you dine in our longhouse," she said.

"Indeed well," he replied.

"And I now must speak to you of something—the reason indeed I have brought you here tonight."

"Ask of me what you will," Tonsahoten answered confidently. He shot a sideways glance at Gandeaktena across the room and hoped no one noticed.

"There are none now in my longhouse or among my kin to defend the honor of this house," she stated gravely, "as well you know. Two nights past, as I lay in my bed and entered the land of dreams, I saw the shades of my ancestors in the spirit world. In one voice they cried out to me that they had deer and corn aplenty, but that their souls still thirsted with a burning heat that no water could quench. For only by devouring the blood of the Fire Nation could their souls be set free from their torments.

"You see, young warrior, that no one of my kin yet lives to answer their plea. So I turn to you to lead a skirmish against the Fire Nation and to return to Oneida with captives to burn."

Silence fell around the crackling fire. The warrior stared into the flames, his eyes stern.

"Thou knowest, aunt," he replied gravely but respectfully, "that I am of the Prayer. Tonsahoten shrinks from no war to which duty calls me. Gladly would I go to war against the Fire Nation if Annonkouaiouton and the *oyander* wished it. But I shall not provoke one afresh, nor will I steal like a fox into the villages and seize a poor soul in the fields on whom you may slake your thirst for vengeance."

The matriarch's visage hardened.

"You are too free in your opinions, warrior, in your refusal of an elder's dream."

"So be it," said he curtly. "But I will not raise my hatchet against the Fire Nation until our captains have declared war."

"Fool!" she upbraided him. "And disrespectful of an elderly woman besides. Do you imagine I am asking your opinion? I am charging you to do this deed for me, to restore the sun in my longhouse. And if you are indeed a man and a warrior you certainly will," and here she pointed a finger at him, "or never will you court my niece."

All eyes were on Tonsahoten, but he turned toward Gandeaktena. She modestly brought her hand to her mouth in embarrassment, and looked around the room, but when she finally looked back at him, she saw he had not broken his gaze toward her. At last, he stood up with smoldering rage, glaring at her adopted aunt.

"Thou hast invited me to thy longhouse to call my bravery into question?" He hurled his kettle into the fire. "Find another murderer to glut thy thirst for blood and to boil and eat the heads of the Fire Nation. There are twenty young men who would. But Tonsahoten utterly and completely refuses."

"And touching the other matter under which thou hast cloaked this nefarious business, I say to thee—thou art for a little while the mistress of Gandeaktena; but her life and the life of Tonsahoten are forever in the hands of the Master of Life. It is Him I obey above all others—and it is to Him I shall make my entreaties. Whatever His will, Tonsahoten is glad to carry it out—but thou art powerless to stop Him."

He stormed out the longhouse.

"An insufferable hothead, that man!" the matriarch sputtered.

But Gandeaktena nursed a newfound respect for the tempestuous warrior and pondered greatly his unswerving loyalty to the Master of Life.

Francis Tonsahoten spoke true, for in time he and Gandeaktena were married. Perhaps this union was promoted by the *agoiander* of Oneida for the legitimate and mutual benefit of its members. Or, perhaps, the elder women had simply amused themselves in joining the fiery, impetuous warrior to the meek, retiring slave. But in any case, many soon found themselves in puzzled admiration of the unlikely spouses.

Francis's temper, his "wayward and capricious" nature, as the Jesuits said of him, served as a whetstone against which Gandeaktena's goodness and virtue were sharpened, and he, in turn, mellowed under "her patience, her sweetness, and her kindness." The mere mention of her name was all it took to soothe his hot blood and quiet the storms that raged within him. But though the Creator had perhaps not favored him with the strictly natural virtues, Francis had been given the supernatural ones of Faith, Hope, and Love, which helped him conform ever more to the model of his crucified Lord.

And the grace of his Baptism was all the more needed now that the men of Oneida were increasingly slipping from the stern, sober example of their grandfathers into a sea of alcoholic decadence. The desire for liquor had become so strong that Oneida men were traveling 200 leagues to buy it openly from the Dutch or from unscrupulous Frenchmen who defied their governor's orders against the trade. Bringing home as much liquor as they could carry, the drunkards would crown their arrival to Oneida with an orgy of gluttony. Violence was sometimes an accidental, and sometimes a very deliberate consequence of these binges.

Either way its perpetrators had a ready excuse prepared to answer for their actions: "What would you have me do? I had no sense—I was drunk."

In the summer of 1667, a brandy-fueled brawl erupted in the town that left four Oneidas dead. Even that tragedy did not chasten the men of the town. The drinking continued, and the violence and the unchastity with it.

While their adopted countrymen sank more deeply into corruption, Francis spoke often to his wife of the Christian faith, and of the manners of the French, with whom he had lived for a time in Quebec. She eagerly drank in his words, especially as he spoke of the Black Robes' doctrines and mysteries of He Who has Made All.

He told her that the great and ineffable Creator had many centuries ago come down to earth, had been born of a Virgin, and had healed the sick and raised the dead. He told her of His death upon the cross, and his rising from the tomb after three days.

"All these things," she said, "are wondrous to hear. You are kindling in me a great desire, husband, to learn more of these mysteries. Would that I might someday learn from the Black Robes as you have!"

While the seasons passed, her fire for the faith only grew.

"I see," Francis said laughing to her one day, after she had bombarded him with questions on a point of doctrine, "that your desire to learn the Prayer of the Black Robes grows greater than my memory can provide. But while we remain here in the midst of drunkards, you will never have your fill of it. Let us resolve, then, to go on the hunt toward Montreal, and from there we will proceed to Quebec to see the castle of the Black Robes. Only there can you find what you have been so long desiring."

In the end, however, this resolution would come to nothing. Before Francis and Gandeaktena could take leave of the lands of the Iroquois, the word had begun to spread through the inhabitants of Oneida castle:

The Black Robes were on their way.

BRUYAS

September, 1667.

The Reverend Father Jacques Bruyas arrived at Oneida in September of 1667. Through his donné Charles
Bocquet, an interpreter who knew a bit of Huron, he gave a
long oration before Annonkouaiouton, the elders, and the
assembled public. He explained that he was a priest sent by the
Master of Life, who had come down to earth many years ago
in a faraway part of the world and had opened to mankind the
door to heaven. This greatest God was, indeed, the only being
truly worthy of their adoration. The other spirits whom their
ancestors had venerated from time immemorial were decep-
tions of the devil, or perhaps devils themselves, and to follow
them was to perish in hell, where there was no remission of
suffering and no hope of escape. But the Master of Life had for
man a great affection, and a fathomless mercy, and He wished
all to abandon their wickedness, turn to Him in supplication,
and to share eternal Life with Him in heaven.

For her part, Gandeaktena grew in wonderment at this
priest as he discoursed about the virtues of the Prayer, and she
listened intently.

A lifetime of stern correction by her kin and then by her
adopted tribe had taught her to view her natural modesty as a
character flaw. Notwithstanding her demure exterior, she had
become a veritable warrior against her own inclinations. But
perhaps the advice of her kinfolk had been wrong all along.
Perhaps her modesty was no unfortunate weakness of her

character—perhaps it was the insistent call of a God who, even in the midst of corruption, decadence, and death, was sweetly coaxing her to ever higher levels of being.

The Black Robe had given Gandeaktena the key to her own soul, and the heavy, debilitating chains of human respect at last began to fall out of her mind. She clearly saw that, whatever the cost, she would strive to learn these mysteries of Prayer, avoid the frightful torments of hell, and gain forever the happiness of Heaven.

"The hunt waits," said Francis to his wife one morning, as he looked over his kit. "I must leave tomorrow."

"Yes," she nodded.

"I have delayed too long for the sake of this Black Robe," he grumbled, strangely angry at himself for his own decision. "But mind that you take good care of him while I am away— he has too few friends in this village."

"I would indeed, yet...." she trailed off.

"Yet what?" he interjected too curtly.

"It would be untoward of me to see him alone."

She was right. He calmed himself and looked up in exasperation.

"Then see that one of your friends takes you, else go with Felicity or one of the Praying Hurons."

"Yes," she nodded. "Yes, I will do that."

"Good." He collected his hunting kit and headed out to procure some added supplies. "And be sure that you learn the Prayers from him," he finished.

Father Bruyas saw a steady stream of visitors in those first days and weeks—mostly out of curiosity and deep disappointment with the deteriorating culture at Oneida. While the village elders had a chapel built for him, one person after another came to visit him in his temporary quarters. And as the older missionaries had warned him, all of the theological training and disputation he had in France proved of little value in his discussion with the Oneida. The native peoples of America had their own particular wisdom and their own particular sets of objections to the Catholic religion—and to these every Jesuit trained on Augustine and Aquinas had to shrewdly adapt.

"In Paradise," one man asked the priest, after a discussion on the glories that awaited the souls of the just, "do they eat bear and moose?"

"If they desire to eat it," the priest replied through his interpreter, "their desires will be satisfied."

"And what of war?" asked a warrior. "Do they go to war in Paradise, and do they kill men and bring home scalps? For without these things, I will not believe."

Bruyas looked perturbed by the question, and wasn't sure how to answer in a way that the interpreter could explain. "If you wish to go to war, you will go; and God will grant you all that you wish." The warrior nodded, apparently satisfied.

Gandeaktena went to see the Black Robe in his public audiences—not as often as she would have liked, but as much as her modesty and her duties in the village would allow her. But she saw, and did not speak. The requests she had made of her friends and relations to accompany her to the priest had all been refused. So she simply sat and listened among all the others, though her heart burned to have a chance to speak to him in private.

Five leagues distant from the town was Lake Oneida. While Tonsahoten and the other men were at the hunt one day, Gandeaktena's adopted aunt had sent her to the fishing grounds along with her mother and several other women. As they came into the town, they were having a lively conversation.

"It cannot be," scoffed Gandeaktena's mother. "He must be here for *some* other reason."

"I do not know," shrugged an Algonquin friend. "I have known many Black Robes. And I tell you, they are not otherwise than what they appear. Poor and unconcerned for the things of the world."

"Well, they are fools then," laughed the Erie. "Let the Andaste come capture him and put him in the kettle. Then we shall see how concerned he is."

The Algonquin laughed as well. "You do not know the Black Robe. I say even *that* would not concern him."

"Kwe kwe!" rang a familiar voice in the distance.

Gandeaktena smiled. "Where are you going, Felicity?"

"To the chapel!"

"The chapel?" she answered with surprise. "Is the Black Robe giving an oration?"

"No!" her friend laughed. "It's time for prayers!"

A Christian Huron, Felicity Gannondadik had volunteered to help Father Bruyas in his mission field. The priest had no knowledge of Oneida and only halting ability in Huron. But she had learned French from the Ursuline nuns in Quebec, so she was serving as his catechist in Oneida, exhorting the catechumens and proselytes and teaching them the essentials of the faith and of prayer. *If I had many like her*, Bruyas wrote to his superior in Quebec, *this whole Village would soon be converted.*

"May I come?!" Gandeaktena asked excitedly, her eyes alight.

"Of course!"

Gandeaktena took her place among the baptized Christians and tried to follow along as best she could. The prayers were in the Huron language, which she knew well, though between the priest's tentative pronunciations and the obscure mysteries they contained, she didn't always understand them.

The prayers having ended, the Hurons began to leave the chapel. But Felicity, who was standing next to Father Bruyas, motioned to Gandeaktena to approach.

"Hello daughter," he said tentatively in Oneida, using one of the few phrases he had picked up so far.

"Hello, Father," she replied in Huron.

"You speak Huron!" he beamed. "You are not Iroquois?"

"I am Erie—the Cat Nation. I was brought here as a girl."

"Ah," said Bruyas thoughtfully, stroking his beard. He had read in the *Relations* of the Cats' downfall.

"And her husband is a Huron," Felicity added in French. "Francis Xavier Tonsahoten. He was baptized by Father Garreau and lived for a while among the French in Quebec."

"Ah...I understand. I understand," he nodded.

"May I stay and learn the Prayer?" Gandeaktena asked, her excitement giving her an uncharacteristic boldness.

"Learn the Prayer." he repeated. "Yes. Stay. Learn."

"May I be Baptized?" she added, with an innocent impertinence.

Father smiled.

"No...not baptized yet....not baptized. First learn."

Gandeaktena nodded.

"She speaks Oneida very well, Father," Felicity interposed. "She has a good ear for it."

The priest brightened. His assigned interpreter, Charles Bocquet, could only manage a little bit of Huron, and he was often away from the village fishing or hunting. Bruyas was left in the village for days hardly able to communicate except to the Huron Christians. Felicity could manage in Oneida, but not well.

"Yes? You teach?" he asked. "Prayer I say Huron, you say Oneida?"

"Yes, Father!" Gandeaktena replied excitedly.

"Good! Tomorrow. Tomorrow."

TWO GREAT AFFLICTIONS

October, 1667.

B ruyas entered the longhouse and came to the fire. He nodded at Gandeaktena and then turned his attention to the
woman lying in the cot. Gandeaktena's adopted aunt had been
ravaged by acute congestion in her chest and repeated attacks
of fever, and the young woman was providing all the physical
and spiritual solace that she could. Surprisingly, she had even
convinced the matriarch to speak to the Black Robe about the
Prayer.

Bruyas studied the patient and felt her forehead. She
looked more like an animated corpse than a living woman;
there would not be much time.

"Aunt," he addressed her. She opened her eyes, saw the
Black Robe and smiled.

"I am glad you are here," she said slowly, as Gandeaktena
translated from Oneida to Huron.

"I am glad as well," Bruyas replied through her niece.
"Do you wish instruction?"

She nodded.

Slowly, and somewhat haltingly, Bruyas then gave a
little oration in Huron about the happiness of believers, and
the joys that the Baptized would enjoy in the life to come.
Gandeaktena rendered all of it into good Oneida, and her
clear mind even supplied for the deficiences in what he could
not say properly. Her aunt listened attentively.

"Do you believe all that I have told you?" the priest asked.

"Yes," she said. "I assuredly do."

Bruyas returned to her several times a day throughout October. She learned well, and she was well taken care of by her adopted niece, but her sickness grew stronger and she grew weaker. She began to ask for Baptism. As the Father saw that her fever was increasing and she was rapidly approaching the end, he agreed.

Gandeakteana's adopted aunt took the Christian name of Agatha.

"Father! Father!" called a voice in Huron outside the chapel.

It was All Saints Day, and Bruyas had had a busy day. He opened the door to see Gandeaktena.

"Yes?"

"Aunt is very sick. She is great pain and cannot speak."

He nodded.

"I will be there."

He came to find Agatha quite pallid on her mat.

"Hello Agatha," he said as he approached. She gave a half smile but it was followed with a wince. Gandeaktena was gently holding her hand. In the other hand, the old woman clutched rosary beads with white knuckles.

"Can she pray?" Bruyas said to Gandeaktena, who translated.

Agatha held her beads up and made the sign of the cross. She raised her eyes to heaven imploringly.

"That is all she can do, Father," her niece said gravely. "She has not spoken since earlier this evening, and now speaks only by signs."

He nodded.

Gandeaktena continued talking to Agatha as she had been before the priest came. She suggested some good thoughts to the dying woman, who listened with great pleasure.

Father Bruyas understood none of it except the often named "Jesus", but he saw the passion and conviction in Gandeaktena's voice, and he saw the effect it was having upon her aunt. He sat back quietly and smiled. There would be time for prayers later.

n the evening of All Souls Day, his Masses finished, Bruyas came to visit Agatha again.

"How is she?" he said to Gandeaktena in Huron.

She gestured to the cot.

"Hello Father," Agatha said raspily.

"Aha!" he smiled. "God has restored your speech!"

But she coughed violently and winced in pain. Her arms sat by her sides. She had not the strength to move them.

Gandeaktena cast her a concerned look.

"Let us say our prayers," Bruyas said quickly, dispensing with pleasantries. He didn't know how much longer she would have her voice.

He pulled out his book and read some appropriate Huron prayers for sickness and for the dying line by line, waiting for Gandeaktena to say them again in Oneida. Agatha repeated the Oneida portion, but only with a great deal of effort. When they finished, she closed her eyes and fell silent with the extreme pain.

After some time, she opened her eyes again and looked at Bruyas, nodding slightly.

He drew out his crucifix.

"Agatha," he said slowly, directly to her as her niece translated, "behold Him who has died to give you life—do you not love Him? Will you still offend Him?"

She stared at the crucifix, and made a final effort to speak.

"Never more any sin; I believe you Jesus, I love you, Jesus, and I shall love you all my life." She reached toward it with her lips.

Bruyas moved the crucifix toward her, and she kissed it with tender devotion. A tear formed on his cheek and on that of her niece.

Agatha passed her last moments in similar acts of love, and then she gave her last sigh and commended her soul to the arms of her Savior.

"So she met a good end." Gandeaktena explained to Francis, who had returned from hunting and was rubbing his sore legs. He was warming himself by their fire in the center of the longhouse as she set the kettle before him.

"Mmm," he nodded, and fell silent for a while. For all the intense friction between the Huron warrior and the Oneida matriarch, he was at least content she had died in the state of grace.

"You brought the priest our extra meat?" he asked.

"Oh yes! He was very grateful for it."

"Good," he nodded.

Gandeaktena sat down with her kettle, made the sign of the cross and said grace in Huron.

Francis crossed himself in surprise, then laughed out loud. "And I see you have not wasted any time learning your prayers!"

She smiled. From outside there were sounds of a commotion in the town. Their neighbors in the longhouse went out to see what was the matter, but Francis and Gandeaktena kept eating.

"It pleases me greatly," he smiled affectionately, "to hear you pray as I do. You will soon surpass your poor husband in prayer, this is certain."

"Oh, nonsense!" Gandeaktena waved off the compliment. He chuckled and finished his sagamite.

By now, the commotion was quite loud and impossible to ignore. Francis craned his neck around to look out of the longhouse. Then a single whoop of triumph went up and the whole village took it up. Gandeaktena shuddered.

The remaining women in her longhouse sprang to their feet.

"Come on!" they urged.

Gandeaktena bit her lip and shook her head. Her kinfolk sneered in disgust and rolled their eyes before leaving.

"I am staying," she stated softly amid the chaos outside.

Francis shrugged and stared at the fire.

Gandeaktena did end up leaving the longhouse, but she avoided the shrieks and the whoops coming from the central plaza and took a roundabout route to the chapel, where she found Father Bruyas. Her face was a twisted knot of confusion and worry.

"Father, is there wrong in going to see captives led into the village? I was resolved not to come out of my house, for fear of displeasing God."

He shook his head, but that was the only answer she got before a fresh round of shouts and yells.

"I may have need of you," he asked earnestly, turning toward the plaza.

Four women had been brought in from the Conestogas from far to the south, near where the Susquehanna River emptied into Chesapeake Bay. Three nations of the Iroquois—the Seneca, Cayuga, and Onondaga—had been fighting a bitter war with the Conestogas since 1661, with heavy casualties and as yet no clear victor on either side. In fact, the two sides had so exhausted themselves by the late 1660s that skirmishes and the seizing of captives, rather than large pitched battles, became the norm. And so a number of young warriors were persuaded to win a cheaper glory, through seizing enemy civilians and bringing them home in false triumph to satiate the bloodlust of their countrymen.

And now, Father Bruyas and Gandeaktena sat before the women from Conestoga. The captives, being allowed a moment of respite, had been badly beaten and had their fingers mauled, burned, and bitten off. They were to be executed that night, so there would be little time for instruction.

Gandeaktena spoke to the petrified captives, and they, sensing some kindness in her, spoke back. But—strangely— no one was able to understand each other. Not Huron, not Oneida, not even her native Erie helped his linguist bridge that barrier.

"Do you not speak their language?"

"No Father. Are you sure they are from Conestoga?"

"That is what the warriors told me," he replied.

She frowned and shook her head. "If they were from Conestoga, I could understand them. This is a completely unknown tongue. They must have been seized from another nation. Perhaps the Conoy, or the Agotzagena along the South River."

"So the warriors lied then," Bruyas shook his head. The Frenchman was disgusted by the practice of seizing civilian prisoners, and he already didn't think very highly of the men who had brought in these captives. And now, it seems, they had not even confined themselves to the true enemy but had gone further afield and seized four innocent women from who knows where. Four women who were now about to be subject to the worst that the Iroquois could inflict.

But—he checked his own thoughts—*that's not going to help these women. I need to do something.*

The women saw he was trying to help them, though they seemed unsure why or how. Their eyes grew more desperate.

"Is there anyone in this village who knows their tongue?" he asked of Gandeaktena impatiently.

She thought for a moment, then left the longhouse and brought back some fellow villagers whom she thought might be helpful. It was no use. Unable to help these poor captives in any way, Bruyas sent her home, where she spent a long night in prayer.

By his own admission, it was the heaviest cross Bruyas had to endure in his entire life to see those four women burned to death before his eyes, as they "cast pathetic and beseeching looks at me from the midst of their flames, as if to ask me for some relief; and to be unable to give them any for either the pains which they suffered then, or those into which they were going to fall."

The next day, Gandeaktena came to see Bruyas again. The catechumen and the priest were both terribly shaken, and his ministrations the night before had made her question her own participation in the grisly scene.

"Father, is there any harm at being present in such executions?" she asked him again.

"You would not offend God if you were present without any motive of hate or vengeance," he replied somberly, "and without taking pleasure in the disgrace of those unfortunates."

"I did not dare to go," she shook her head slowly. "For fear of displeasing God."

CATECHUMEN &
COMPANION

December, 1667.

Father Bruyas called Felicity aside after prayers one day. "Gandeaktena has asked again about Baptism," Bruyas said. "She desires it greatly, and I wish to grant it to her. But I must not be imprudent in this regard. What can you tell me of her?"

Since the priest had been at Oneida, he had baptized only children and adults in danger of death. And having seen first hand the free and easy divorces that prevailed there, he had demanded a longer catechumenate for those who were married.

"She has never, Father, that I know of, violated her fidelity to her husband. And she has certainly been importuned to do so."

His eyebrows raised.

"Indeed?"

"The licentious do not spare even her from their advances—sometimes I even think they look upon her as the greatest conquest of all, if only to place a black mark on her piety."

"Hmph," Bruyas said with disgust. In that respect, they were little different from many like-minded Frenchmen he knew. But unlike the French, it was almost unheard of for an Iroquois to commit such an unmanly act as to take a woman by force. Whatever their faults, these infidels had better kept this particular tenet of the moral Law than the Christians of

Europe who had not only Nature but Holy Mother Church to guide them.

Cui multum datum est multum quaeretur ab eo, he thought. To whom much has been given, much will be required.

"There has been a great deal of witchery directed to her as well, Father."

"Eh? Witchery?"

"Some of the women have put the medicine-men up to it. They have cast spells upon her that she be rendered barren."

Bruyas shook his head. Francis and Gandeaktena had had no children in the few years they had been married, and in her conversations with her, she had admitted it was a great source of shame to her, and even a temptation to doubt the Providence of God.

"She will be in need of our prayers. The Devil has taken notice of her."

Certainly, that was true; the legions of hell were losing a soul. Gandeaktena grew ever greater in the practice of the faith. She attended the Prayers regularly and easily learned them along with the others. Her conscience grew ever more delicate, to the point where she would hardly undertake some significant action without asking the priest if there were anything wrong in it.

Yet in other ways, she grew ever more bold. The young woman who made such an effort to overcome her natural inclinations of modesty for the sake of peace in the village was now increasingly open with her acts of piety—no matter the irreligiousness of her audience. Her relatives and many others in the village certainly noticed. And many of them resented it.

"You are hastening your own death! Do you not see how many people Baptism has killed since the Black Robe came to this village? This belief has already killed dozens—and it will not spare you either, we assure you."

"When I see," Gandeaktena replied adamantly, "that those who do not believe do not die, I will listen to your remonstrances. Until then, you will not change my mind in the least."

⊨⊨⊨⊨ ✝ ⊨⊨⊨⊨

After their evening meal, Francis Xavier reclined on his furs. His legs were still inexplicably paining him since his return from the hunt—a sharp, unusual pain which was not typical of fatigue. Gandeaktena massaged them with bear grease, which gave him a little relief, though not much.

"The black robe's young companion is being sent to Quebec," he said dispassionately, "and he will be in need of guides. I have put myself at the disposal of the *oyander* in this matter."

She nodded. "Do what you must do."

"I have it in mind to find some remedies for my legs," he continued, "in the hospital of Montreal."

"It is a good idea."

He studied her face, but he saw there no ill feelings about his announcement. Perhaps now that the black robes had come to Oneida, she had forgotten about going to Quebec.

He thought about it for a while longer. There was no need to make a decision now. He would wait a few days.

⊨⊨⊨⊨ ✝ ⊨⊨⊨⊨

Father Bruyas was making the most of a cold rainy evening by composing a letter by candlelight to his superior, when Gandeaktena came to visit.

"Come in," he motioned. The chapel was dim, and the raindrops rapped on the bark roof.

"Kwe, Father."

"Kwe," he smiled in return. "It pleases me that your husband will accompany Bocquet to Quebec."

"He was one of the first to volunteer," she replied.

"I would expect nothing less of Francis," he smiled. "But are you to go with him as well?"

"No, no, not I," she answered.

The priest was greatly relieved. He could afford to lose Bocquet but not Gandeaktena. And he had started to hope that she would be the pillar around which he could build the Church in Oneida.

"Father," she asked him with a note of concern, "I am troubled by something."

"Tell me," he replied, motioning her to be seated.

She did so, settling her skirt neatly on the ground. "It is a great thing, Father, to learn the mysteries of Prayer, and I thank the Master of Life every day that He took pity on this poor slave and sent the Black Robes here to teach me. I would that all of Oneida be converted—but I see too that it has become a town given over to licentiousness. If only I were a better Christian, Father, my example could perhaps serve to turn the ways of the wicked. But I fear for my soul here. At every turn the demon lies in wait to snare me. I fear that in a moment of weakness I will succumb to some great temptation for drink or impurity, or that some great misfortune befall me and that I give in to the entreaties of the medicine-men."

Bruyas nodded in understanding, but his heart sank.

"And I wish greatly, Father, to live with those who worship God as I do. Among true Christians where vice is not known."

If his countrymen deserved such an overoptimistic characterization, Bruyas did not know it. But her remark was born of a holy innocence, so he let it stand.

"It is as you say here," he replied. "But you mistake, Gandeaktena, in mistrusting He Who Has Made All. If it is His will to keep you in this village amidst the profligates, He will not abandon you. He will lavish upon you all the helps needed to secure your salvation in spite of it. I do not say you are wrong to want to go and live with the French—indeed, it may be that God prepares your heart for it even now. But if at this moment it is His will for you to remain at Oneida, do not waste that time. Live as best you can here where He has seen fit to place you, and do not spend your thoughts idly on opportunities that have not yet arisen."

"You are right," she nodded slowly. "You are right." She got up, bade the priest a good night, and then drew a mantle over her head and walked out into the wet night.

Bruyas tried to continue his letter but soon put his quill down, distracted. He could not argue with Gandeaktena's conclusion. As personally aloof as she kept from the madness around her, how many times in France and in Canada had he sternly advised penitents to avoid the near occasion of sin? Here now was a whole town full of it, and even he was not immune to its sickly sweet poison, notwithstanding the method St. Ignatius had bequeathed to the members of his order to systematically train their wills.

Alone in the chapel, the Black Robe continued to worry himself until he finally stretched out his hands toward the heavens.

"Lord, this mission was undertaken for Thy glory alone. And with great pains Thou hast secured but a few successes. Is it now Thy Will to take from me my interpreters, and leave me a dumb lamb among wolves?"

The rain continued to fall against the bark roof.

On the eve of his departure, Gandeaktena was helping her husband prepare, thinking deeply about what Father had told her. Tonsahoten watched her fill a pouch with dried venison and cornmeal.

"Two."

She looked up at him.

"What?"

"Pack for two."

She looked down at the pouch, then back at him.

"It is my wish that you come with me," he explained. "We will go together to visit the French, as once we had decided."

Her heart leapt.

"I am quite prepared to go," she beamed, "but I told the Black Robe I was to stay."

"Is that a sin?" Tonsahoten answered curtly. "I had not yet asked you."

She nodded, but now that the opportunity to see the French had come so unexpectedly, she could think only of what she was leaving behind.

"I will go with you, husband. Gladly will I go. I will give my farewell to my mother, and then I must see the Black Robe."

"So suddenly??" Gandeaktena's mother gasped.

"He only told me this evening," she answered patiently.

"Dearest, I do not know why you would subject yourself to a man's whims like this. Any normal woman would say 'no' and let that be the end of it."

Her daughter stayed silent. Gandeaktena's marriage was a mystery to her mother, as it was to most people in the village.

"It will be Spring before I see you again," she added.

"Or you may come with us, if you wish."

"I am old, Gandeaktena, too old for great journeys. Everything I have left in this world is here, and what goes on in the castles of the French does not interest me. Go. Winter among them. Do not forget your poor mother at Oneida."

"How could I, mother?" Gandeaktena replied with tears, kissing her head.

Very early the next morning, she told Father Bruyas of Tonsahoten's decision. He had resigned himself to this eventual fate several days ago, but that didn't make its suddenly coming true any easier. He was losing not only his primary linguistic link to the Oneida, but also a dear friend.

"Do not pity your poor Father," he said bravely, "who must learn even more now to trust in God and not to his own abilities. If God wills it, I will manage here. If God wills otherwise, then my great failure on earth will be my crown of obedience in heaven. Go, Gandeaktena. Accompany your husband. See for yourself the society of Christians. See the great Churches raised to God, see the holy nuns, and all the great ceremonies of the Church. And do not fail to pray."

"Oh no, Father, how could I?!" she replied, horrified.

He laughed.

"Is Francis at home? I would come and bestow upon you the Church's blessing."

"He is, thank you, Father!"

She returned to her longhouse alone, and a few minutes later Father Bruyas arrived.

Scattered across a log table were several purses full of necklaces, wampum and glass beads, and other ornaments. Gandeaktena was sorting through the contents with her mother.

Whatever Francis Xavier's moody nature, he had been an excellent provider to his young wife. His hunting skills had kept the family well stocked with meat, and thanks to his leadership and the warriors' respect accorded him by the other men of Oneida, much else besides.

Gandeaktena had won the men's respect as well. Her part of the longhouse was always open to visitors seeing her husband, and they appreciated her feminine modesty and her cheery eagerness to share with them the bounty of her husband's hunt and her own garden's produce. In fact, the men seemed to appreciate her more than the women of the village, who had grown jealous of how quickly the former slave had come into new-found wealth. The very women who had plotted and laughed at the marriage of the shy captive to the fierce Huron warrior were not laughing now.

"God has certainly blessed you," Bruyas said cheerily.

"I was just getting rid of some of this finery," she replied in embarrassment.

"You are being unreasonable," her mother added. "Will you not have need of them in Quebec?"

"I have found something of greater value."

Her mother shook her head dismissively.

"But take *something*, no?"

"I will—" she said weakly, motioning toward two purses on the far corner of the table. "this one and this one. And everything that belongs to Francis. The rest I will not need. Let them find a better use among you here in Oneida."

Her mother shrugged, and began collecting the rest of the purses as Francis Xavier walked up from the other side of the longhouse.

"We are ready, Father," Gandeaktena said.

The priest pulled out his prayer book.

"Good. Let us begin."

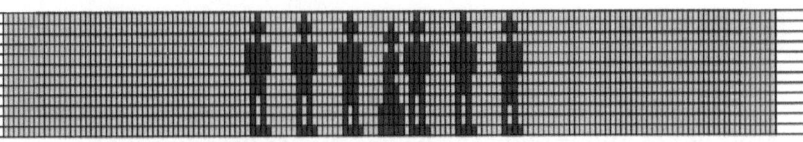

SEVEN ACROSS THE ICE

Six Oneida in all journeyed north to Montreal with Boc-quet through the creaking woods. In Iroquois-style snow-shoes and leggings amid the December snows, their torsos were wrapped tightly in mantles to stave off the bitter winds. Gandeaktena led them in their Huron prayers every day as they huddled by the campfires with their backs to boulders or as they trudged over snowbanks and dimly lit hills, until they reached the great St. Lawrence river and walked over its frozen surface to the island of Montreal.

Jeanne Mance, foundress and former head of the Ho-tel-Dieu, the hospital of Montreal, was preparing lists of needed items in her personal quarters when a knock sounded on the door.

"Enter."

A nun came in. Her given name was Judith Moreau de Bresoles, one of three Religious Hospitallers of St. Joseph whom the foundress had brought from France in 1659.

"Mademoiselle Mance, Charles Bocquet has arrived from the Iroquois with an embassy."

"Thank you, Sister. I will be there shortly."

Mademoiselle Mance put her quill back into the inkstand and squinted over her last list. There was much she yet needed to write. But an injury had left her without the use of her right arm, and it was exasperating to write with her left. Also, she was eager for news from Bocquet and did not want to keep him waiting. The travelers would be exhausted from their journey and in need of shelter and food.

She stood slowly from her chair, sighing at her uncooperative bones and leaving the papers on her desk for later.

While Bocquet and the six Oneida warmed themselves by the fireplace of the Hospital, in came a gray-haired woman of about 60 years, with suffering but also a great kindness in her face.

"Monsieur Bocquet!" she greeted him, as he gave her an affectionate embrace.

As the two conversed in French, Gandeaktena gazed around her. The Hospital was a wooden construction of two floors. Much of the space served as a room for the sick, and rather than central fires, there were stone fireplaces at each end.

"...and these are my traveling companions from Oneida." Bocquet suddenly said in Huron, reclaiming her attention. "My friends, this is the Mademoiselle Mance, foundress of the Hospital" Mademoiselle Mance greeted them warmly. "They are all good Christians," he added in French, "and they have passed the journey in constant prayer."

"Very good, very good!" Mance said to the party in Huron. "How good that you are here for Christmas! Father Rafeix arrives in a few days."

Rafeix was wintering across from the Isles Percees at the farm of Pierre Boucher. He had been sent there to investigate some land across from Montreal Island at La Prairie de la Magdelaine, which had just been titled to the Jesuits. He and the other Jesuits already had an office in the Hospital, and a little chapel that served as the parish church for the settlers of Montreal island.

"Mademoiselle," continued Bocquet in French, gesturing toward Tonsahoten, "I will especially commend to your care this man here, whose name is Francis Xavier Tonsahoten. He has come expressly to the Hospital to seek some remedies for the pains in his legs. He is a Huron who was baptized before the war by our Fathers in his own country."

"Do your legs pain you much?" she asked Tonsahoten in Huron.

He nodded.

"The holy virgins will see if there is anything to be done," she added, using the typical Huron expression for the Hospital nuns. "Meanwhile, warm yourselves while I bring you all something from the kitchen."

Gandeaktena smiled at her husband, and he smiled back. It had taken them a long time, but the first step of their journey was complete.

As she had done with increasing frequency at Oneida, Gandeaktena attended the Hospital chapel and participated in the church ceremonies as far as she was able.

And she was rewarded in these few weeks with an enormous outpouring of grace. The splendid Masses of Advent at Montreal began to banish the sordid life of Oneida from her mind, as the rays of a glorious and happy dawn dissipate forever the dark and confused emotions of a bad dream. She now understood what Father Bruyas must have known all along—that the private liturgies he had offered in the bark chapel at Oneida were only dim copies of what the French did every day in their parish churches. "Karonhiage," she sobbed to Francis Xavier one Sunday, with tears streaming down her face after the schola chanted the *Sanctus* and the French all dropped to their knees in adoration: "it is heaven." Her soul took flight above her, reeling in the beauty of the Mass and the intimacy of her Creator, to so condescend to man as to lay down His own precious Body for their spiritual food.

In Montreal the worship of the Master of Life was no furtive, covert action of a few outcasts, but the central focus of an entire society. Here, those who held most fast to the Prayer were not jeered at and mocked but lauded and honored. The sweet air of freedom intoxicated the former slave with a peace she had not felt since before the war, when she played in the lap of her father at Gentaienton. All that was good about those days seemed now reborn here at Montreal.

Her husband, however, was becoming restless. The treatments for his legs had helped, but they were being sheltered from the cold Canadian December in the Hospital, and living off the generosity of the French was eating away at the proud warrior's heart. Often he would wander alone from the Hospital, breathe in the bitingly crisp air, and gaze out over the frozen St. Lawrence. He surveyed the terrain with the eyes of a hunter and warrior, longing to lose himself in the snow-covered wilderness on some grand and daring adventure. He had left Oneida an honored and respected man, only to be now no better than a pauper.

He shook his head, and prayed toward the ice-cold heavens. "Lord, this is no life for a warrior."

Father Pierre Rafeix arrived, as promised, in a few days. He made a special point to visit the travelers from Oneida, and he came to them with an offer.

"The Great Captain of the French has given to the Black Robes a tract of land at La Prairie on the other side of the river. It has lain unused during the war with the Iroquois. But the peace has now brought me here from Montreal to oversee its settlement."

"It is beautiful land," replied Tonsahoten. "I have often seen it from the island."

"It is indeed," the priest replied. "Over the summer our Frenchmen have been employed in clearing it. At present, there is only one cabin built—a simple shed of boards. Here our Frenchman are now wintering—but there will be sufficient room for all of you as well. And you will no longer need to stay at the Hospital."

Tonsahoten nodded stoically, though very pleased.

"Very well, Father. Give me leave to consider it, and I will give you my answer this evening."

Later, the Oneida travelers attended the Mass of the Christmas Vigil, when Holy Mother Church burst forth in exuberant praise for the Christ child, the Son of God come into the world a tiny helpless babe in the simple poverty of Bethlehem. Gandeaktena's heart sang at the sight of the creche and its little figurines so realistically rendered in the European manner and set with such tender expressions of love.

Dearest child, she thought in tears as she gazed upon the Savior in the manger, *if it be Thy will that my womb never bear its string of children, come possess my heart, and I will nurse you there with all the love I have.*

After Mass, Tonsahoten met with Father Rafeix and accepted his offer. He then led his wife and the five other Oneida across the ice once more, to live among the French at La Prairie. Or, as they would come to know it, *Kentake*: "at the meadow."

BY THE HANDS
OF THE BISHOP

The happy winter of 1667–1668 was, for Gandeaktena, a schooling in the culture of Christendom. Not just the doctrines and the dogmas, not just the sacraments and mysteries, but a deeper and fuller Christian life that colored the entire rhythm of the year with the Gospel of Christ. The Iroquois, after all, were no strangers to seasonal observances, and they did not hold to the folly of a purely mental, intellectual religion. They had kept their Strawberry festival, that Gandeaktena so loved, and others from time immemorial before the French had ever arrived at these shores.

It is natural to man—and even more so the religious man—to keep a cycle of devotions to be acted in harmony with the rhythms of the natural world. So it was an aspect of Iroquois religion as natural as rain or wind—one not to abandoned even as the saving Gospel had spread among the sons and daughters of Aataensic.

But none of the Oneida, not even Francis Xavier Tonsahoten among the Hurons, had ever experienced a culture so thoroughly and deeply Christian as they had among the French at La Prairie. By imitating their example, and under Father Rafeix's pastoral care, Gandeaktena and her companions at La Prairie grew in knowledge and love for the faith.

La Prairie, April 2, 1668. Easter Monday.

"It is all arranged," Father Rafeix told Francis Xavier and his wife, relishing a hearty meal of meat after the austerity of the Lent just passed. The bitter cold of Canada had made him far more appreciative of the breaking of fasts.

"Bocquet will leave for Quebec in a few days and give his report of the Oneida mission. All that needs to be done now is to accompany him to see the Bishop. His Grace will speak to you in person and you may well have the privilege to receive the sacrament from Monseigneur himself."

Gandeaktena felt a twinge of nervousness at the prospect of meeting a successor of the Apostles. "Am I ready, Father?"

He laughed, and her husband could not suppress a smirk.

"If you are not, then none are. But Father Chaumonot will see to your continued instruction at Quebec. I cannot believe you will return here a heathen," he concluded with a smile.

"It is my wish we do not stay long," interjected Francis Xavier, suddenly cross.

"Mmm," Rafeix nodded. He had no words to assuage the warrior's pride in this matter—and perhaps God had His own reasons for wanting him so humbled.

"Is it still your wish, Francis, to settle among the Hurons at Quebec?"

"We shall see," he replied. "I have been too long away from my kin, and I fear I have become too Iroquois by temperament."

"Pay a call to Father Chaumonot. I'm sure he would smooth the way with your kin if you had it in your heart to live there. They are even now preparing to leave the fort and settle in the woods a league and half away. But, if you do not wish it that is another matter."

Francis Xavier nodded.

Quebec. April 11, 1668.

"Monseigneur?"

François Montmorency de Laval, Vicar Apostolic of New France and Bishop of Petraea, looked up from his desk.

"Bocquet has arrived with a delegation from Oneida."

"Ah. Splendid. Send them in right away." He rubbed his eyes. This morning he was eager for distraction—he had been shoring up plans for a Minor Seminary that was due to open later in the year.

The messenger bowed and scampered away, returning a moment later with the travelers.

"Monseigneur!" Bocquet bowed grandly and kissed the bishop's hand. The Oneida followed, though awkwardly.

"I have long awaited news from the Iroquois, Monsieur Bocquet," the bishop answered. "It pleases me beyond words to see you."

"And I you, Monseigneur."

"But first," he said, his eyes beaming, "you must tell me of these first fruits of the mission! I understand we have Christians here in all but name."

"This, Monseigneur, is the leader of our pious band of Iroquois: Francis Xavier Tonsahoten. He is a Huron by nation, and was baptized by Fr. Garreau. His wife here, Gandeaktena, was a slave of the Cat Nation, and she took most excellent care of Father Bruyas."

"Splendid, splendid," the bishop beamed. "The Cat Nation. What a great pity we had no Fathers to send to them while they yet stood. Are there any more of her tribe remaining?" he asked Bocquet, who relayed the question to Gandeaktena and translated her answer.

"Yes, Monseigneur, her mother still lives at Oneida and there are others among the Iroquois as well. The rest are said to have fled to the south to Virginia and the English."

"Then the ruin of her country has proved her blessing,"

replied the bishop, "to have removed her from the sway of heathens and heretics."

"This is a grand reunion, Tonsahoten," said a familiar face at Lorette, as he embraced his friend warmly. "We have seen many Iroquois pass by here of late, and I knew within my heart that one day you would be among them."

Paul Honoguenhag had, like many Hurons since the fall of their nation, lived for many years among the Iroquois and to a certain extent had adopted their ways. There he came to know Francis Xavier well. The two had always shared the same boldness of heart, but Paul's gifts were those of rhetoric and wisdom rather than the hunt and war.

They caught up on old news over a meal and then Paul led Francis around Fort Ste. Louis, which Governor Ailleboust had built for the Hurons' protection after the Iroquois incursions on Quebec. The whole settlement was a hive of activity, in preparation for its relocation.

"Among the Iroquois we lived as an enslaved, shattered people. Here we live as free men."

"Free men?" Francis replied sarcastically. "in a makeshift camp built within the palisades of the French and behind their guns?"

"We were five years upon the island. But in the main, yes. As long as the Iroquois were harassing the settlements, we had little choice."

Francis scowled.

"Now that they have sued for peace," Paul quickly added, "we are leaving for a new site about a league from here—the Black Robes call it Our Lady of the Snows."

"How many are you?"

"Two hundreds perhaps."

"And are there French there?"

"It is a French settlement, yes," Paul answered cautiously.

"Listen to me Paul," Francis said too angrily. "You cannot live as the French forever."

"Do you think that is our intent?" Paul answered, restraining his own sternness. "We will have our own village there. We will support ourselves. Our own land. Our own fields."

"Fields?" replied Francis. "Fields that the women will tend, or the men?"

Now Paul scowled. Among the Indians, farming was traditionally women's work—and though many of the nations were warming to French custom in this regard, it was still considered a demeaning occupation for a warrior.

"Francis," he replied, "your mind is crooked. Do you not remember eight years ago, when Anahotaha took 40 of the best Huron warriors on the warpath against seven hundreds of Iroquois, and they were cut down and burnt defending this settlement?"

"I do remember," Francis nodded. "I myself saw the captives led to Onondaga."

"Then do not darken what little sun remains for these people. They are reduced and broken, and they do what is necessary to live. They cannot seize captives to replenish their ranks, and must rely solely on what the Master of Life grants them"

Francis shook his head.

"But let us speak no more of it." Paul concluded. "Come. Let us find your wife, and pay a visit to the Black Robe."

Father Pierre Joseph-Marie Chaumonot was a veteran of the Canadian missions who was said to know the Huron language better than the Hurons themselves. He interviewed

Gandeaktena for a long time, and he found it remarkable that she had come to him so well prepared to be worthy of the waters of Christian regeneration. He set out, in the ensuing days, to complete what Father Bruyas and Father Rafeix began, and in a short time, she was deemed ready.

By the hands of François Montmorency de Laval, Vicar Apostolic of New France and Bishop of Petraea, Gandeaktena of Gentaienton was solemnly baptized into Holy Mother the Church, taking the Christian name of Catherine.

She was then anointed with the chrism of Confirmation, and finally, Francis Xavier Tonsahoten and Catherine Gandeaktena knelt within the hallowed bounds of the sacristy to pronounce their vows before the bishop and be joined in the grace of a sacramental Matrimony.

B ack at the mission, a celebratory feast was offered for the newly baptized. But as the sun fell in the skies over the tables of the Hurons, Francis Xavier Tonsahoten and Paul Honoguenhag walked out of the mission into the surrounding woods, as his wife followed them.

"You told me once my mind was crooked touching this mission," Francis said to Paul, "But nonetheless, it offers no life for me. I cannot continue to live on alms or break the soil. My heart longs for the hunt and for the warpath. I am not an Apostle to go from town to town begging for my bread."

"No," Paul agreed. "You are not. But you profess the Prayer. And you would do well to remain with those who profess it also, and not the wicked who scorn it."

"Be that as it may. I have no intention to live here. None whatever."

"Shall we return to Oneida?", his wife interposed.

He turned to her with eyes wide.

"Return? You have had it in your heart for so long to live among Christians, and now you would return to live amongst the infidels?"

"Oh no, Francis, not to live, no. But how could we receive so great a gift from the hands of the bishop, and not desire the same for our kin? How could we live with such joy, knowing that our relatives suffer among the heathen? I wish to return to Oneida not to remain but to persuade my mother and your father to return to Quebec with us."

His visage turned dark. "You mock me woman! To secure these blessings for our kin is one thing—but to return to live at Quebec? What have I here any longer?!"

She took a deep breath. "I would never mock you," she said patiently, in a soothing tone. "But I fear the fickle Oneida—that before long, they will cast the Black Robes out again and return to ways even more impious than before."

"Fear it?" Paul added, "It is almost certain, from what I have heard. The drink rules Oneida now. And the miserable Dutch heretics every day bend their ears against the Fathers."

"Then why, husband, can we not remain with Paul and the Hurons at Quebec? I ask not to anger you, still less to mock, but only to understand."

"I am Iroquois, Gandeaktena," he shouted, as if he were disclosing some hidden vice. "It is as simple as that. I have become an Iroquois."

He was silent for a moment, and then began again passionately.

"If we were to leave this place now, flee south through the mountains and return to the fires of the Cats, what would you say of it?"

Catherine looked to heaven. That life was long behind her, and it had been many years since she had wished to rejoin her countrymen. True, that she often daydreamed of those summers of her youth, that she treasured them as a precious heirloom within her memory. But in her memory they must forever remain, for her father and most of her kin were dead, Gentaienton was undoubtedly an overgrown ruin, and her mother and friends now lived in the Iroquois cantons. Whatever survived of her nation in the south held little interest for her.

"Do you see?" Tonsahoten said forcefully. "What do the fires of the Huron have for me any longer? My former countrymen are planters and fishermen. I have become too Iroquois in temperament, too accustomed to grand deeds to return to a people so humiliated and wasted. Shall I cease sharpening my arrows and take to the corn fields? Shall I lay aside my bow for a net and a fish-gig?"

"I do see," Catherine replied. "I do see." She looked up toward the stars. "What, then, if we leave Quebec tomorrow and return to our kin at Oneida? We shall persuade them to come with us, and along the way we shall pray to He Who Has Made All, that He direct us whithersoever He will."

He nodded, and gave a little smile.

"It is well. By the summer's end, we shall be once again in Oneida."

The will of Providence, however, had decreed otherwise.

Their canoe gliding up the St. Lawrence River, Francis Xavier and Catherine paddled toward Montreal as the first building came into view.

She paused and turned around toward her husband at the stern. "Toward the hospital?"

"La Prairie," Francis Xavier corrected, motioning with his head toward the south bank. She switched the paddle to her right.

When they arrived, Catherine stepped out into the shallow water and carried paddles and packs toward the land.

Francis Xavier paddled a few more feet until the bow grounded, and then he pushed the boat onto the shore.

"Kwe!! Kwe!!" shouted someone in the distance.

The warrior's brow furrowed, and he shot a glance further up the shore. On the edge of the woods stood an old man waving his arms and walking towards them. Catherine stopped where she was, looking back toward the canoe. Francis Xavier held his hand out and gestured for her to not go any further. He scanned the surrounding woods for signs of an ambush—if need be they could be back on the water in seconds and might well make it to the fort without being overtaken.

"Kwe!" he shouted back.

As the stranger neared, some peculiar characteristic of the old man's gait caused Francis to squint in disbelief. Then his face lit up in a broad smile.

"My father!" he called out, laughing.

The old man stopped, shielding his eyes from the sun.

"It is I, father!" Francis laughed, throwing his paddle down and running to greet him.

"Tonsahoten! Gandeaktena!" his father laughed. He turned toward the woods, calling, "Come out, come out!"

Catherine raced to her father-in-law. Then she saw her mother come out of the woods and ran to embrace her as well, this time covered in joyous tears.

In the end, no return to Oneida was necessary. Everyone they were going to bring was already here—having come to hunt in the vicinity but no doubt also inspired by an interior grace. The travelers spent the night at La Prairie catching up on all the news at Oneida and among the French.

"It is a most beautiful river," Catherine's mother told her as they enjoyed a walk together at dusk along the St. Lawrence. She sighed. Something else was on her mind as well.

"I see now, daughter, what I have not seen clearly before."

"Oh?"

"At Oneida, the women's tongues wagged day and night about you and your husband. Witches continued to cast all manner of spells against you. And I had feared, as long as you were barren, that these spells had found their mark, and that an evil spirit had come to possess you both."

Catherine cast her eyes downward.

"But I am certain they have not," her mother stated. "My mind was crooked about Tonsahoten. Tempestuous and stubborn he may be, but he is as good a man as can be found throughout the whole of Oneida. When the two of you departed, it was if the sun had been extinguished in the sky. All of my life there turned dark, and I took no more pleasure in it. I remembered how content you were to pray and to commend yourself to He Who Has Made All. So to Him I, too, commended myself. And in Him I found a great peace. It was surely He who had protected you from all the calumnies and sorceries of the jugglers. And it was surely He who directed us hither and brought us to meet upon the river."

Catherine wiped away a tear. "So happy you have made me!"

"And do not be ashamed," her mother admonished. "He is Master over us all and beside him the jugglers of Oneida and the evil *oki* are but nothing. As firmly as I believe in Him, I believe that He will lift this weight upon you. Do you remember what your father said to you, long ago? You will be a mother yet, Gandeaktena. You will be a mother yet."

They embraced again in tears.

After they rejoined the others, Francis Xavier and Catherine tried to persuade their relatives to go to Quebec to see Father Chaumonot and be baptized.

"I do not deny," said Francis's father, "that my heart longs for the joy you have gained there."

"Then what is to be said more about the matter?" replied Francis Xavier passionately. "All that you seek is in Quebec." Catherine's mother shook her head. "I am an old woman, and it is only with great difficulty that I have traveled this far."

"And every day that passes you shall be older and the difficulty greater still," the warrior answered impertinently. "And at its greatest, that difficulty will be little as compared to the tortures of the damned."

She glared at him.

"Even so, my son," Tonsahoten's father interposed, "we are utterly unacquainted with Quebec. We are strangers in a strange land, without anyone to accompany us thither or to receive us when we arrive."

"Then come with me," Catherine spoke up, "and I will render this favor to you complete. I will gladly bear you company."

Francis's father looked pensive for a moment. He surveyed the faces of his companions, who waited for him to make the decision.

"It would be a great kindness, Gandeaktena. But have you not just this day come from there? Will you now retrace every one of your steps just made?"

"I do not believe them lost," she replied, "since they are employed for so good an end."

After some time at La Prairie, the entire band of about a dozen made the journey to Quebec. Father Chaumonot again assumed responsibility for instructing the new group of refugees, and by the end of the summer they, too, received Baptism by the hands of the bishop of New France. But though Paul Honoguenhag, the missionary, and others at the Huron mission still cherished hopes of retaining their new converts at Quebec, Francis Xavier had no intention of staying.

As autumn chilled the air and painted the leaves of Canada in gold, red and orange, the Huron warrior led his little band back up the St. Lawrence River again.

THE CABIN
BY THE TURTLE

When they arrived at Montreal, Francis Xavier was still uncertain about where to settle. The life of the hunt and the warpath appealed to his thoughts once more, and he again considered resuming his life at Oneida.

His wife, however, gently persuaded him to at least remain among the French, and in the end he saw the advantage in it. They would winter at La Prairie with Father Rafeix , who had room for the whole little band.

"And now," Francis Xavier declared triumphantly once they had settled, "we shall waste no more time. We leave for the hunt."

Into the woods around Montreal he plunged the able-bodied members of his band with great fervor, his warrior's heart replenished by the ambush, the chase over hill and stream, the chilly nights by the fire under the trees and the stars.

Catherine and the others responded to the grace of their recent Baptism with similar zeal. Every morning and evening they were assiduous in saying their prayers, consecrating their days to God. Father Rafeix had given them a parting gift as they had gone into the woods—a carved stick on which he had marked all the Sundays and major feast days. By means of this woodland calendar, they kept holy Our Lord's Day and knew when to return to the village for Mass with the French on Christmas and the other great feasts.

This particular hunt proved unsuccessful, owing to the short time they spent in the woods. But the little band of

Christian Oneida had won something far greater than the fruit of the chase. In their material poverty, they had grown in the faith, and began a practice of pursuing holiness that would continue for years to come.

Meanwhile, Father Rafeix was overseeing the preparation of the land at La Prairie for a more permanent settlement. Fields were cleared and plots were marked out. Francis Xavier chose a plot upriver from La Prairie along a tributary called La Tortue, "the Turtle", and there he built a cabin for his family.

God blessed this new home with every good, material and spiritual. The Oneida sowed their corn in the newly plowed fields, and it grew quickly and richly in the fertile fields. The Riviere de la Tortue was full of trout and eel, and the hunting in the surrounding woods, after that first inauspicious venture, proved excellent.

Every morning and every evening, Catherine led the band in its prayers in the Huron language, and the others repeated after her. They devoutly attended Father Rafeix's Masses with the French in the little wooden cabin at La Prairie.

The blessings showered upon this little band could not long stay quiet, and soon knowledge of this longhouse of Christian Iroquois spread up the St. Lawrence toward the country of the Ottawa and even down to the country of the Five Nations.

July 28th, 1669.

The great feast of St. Anne, beloved by the Canadian French, had been celebrated with great fervor with solemn Mass at La Prairie on the Sunday following the feast. Father Rafeix's homily had been on St. Joachim and St. Anne's charity, and the disposition of their worldly goods into three parts: one part for God's service in the temple, one part for the poor, and one part for they themslves to live on.

That afternoon, Catherine took out the two deerskin purses of beads and necklaces she had brought from Oneida. She emptied them both out on the table, and divided them into three piles.

"What are you doing?" Francis Xavier wandered over, eating some corn bread with raspberries baked into it.

"St. Anne," she replied.

"What about St. Anne?"

"I have been thinking about Father's homily."

"And?"

"Dividing her earthly goods into three parts, for the poor, for the Temple, and for her family."

"Ah..." he nodded. "Yes, I remember. So you wish to do the same?"

She nodded. He saw that his own wampum belts and war decorations were not on the table.

"Just check with Fr. Rafeix first."

"Of course," she replied.

Father Rafeix gave his consent with great pleasure—perhaps in part because his homily had found such an eager imitator. So Catherine walked briskly back home, replaced the third pile in one of the purses, then carefully pushed the rest of the material into the second purse and brought it to the chapel.

She was relieved to see the chapel was empty, except for the Sanctuary light and the Blessed Sacrament. She crossed herself at the door and set herself down in the middle of the nave.

"My God," she prayed, laying the overflowing purse on the floor. "You have blessed me with so much in this world—

my husband, my kin, and all of this finery that I have brought here before you. And though I was undeserving, you gave me all these riches to use in my life. I thank you, with all of my heart. And after the example of good Sts. Anne and Joachim, I wish you to receive this finery back from me, and use it wherewith to feed your poor and to build your church.

"But more than that, Lord. I want to offer to you my body, and I offer to you my soul. Whatever I can accomplish for Thee in this life, whatever my poor hands and heart can do for you, I give gladly and freely, as an instrument for Thy holy will."

As she concluded her prayer, she crossed herself again, and rose to bring these gifts to Fr. Rafeix.

Late Summer, 1669.

"Catherine," Francis stuck his head in the cabin, as she looked up from her needlework. "A traveler has arrived. From Onondaga."

She nodded and set down her thread and cloth. Providence had blessed Francis with a successful hunt when he had gone into the woods to provide for some Frenchmen who were staying with them. There would certainly be enough for another guest as well.

"We will be ready," she replied, and began to prepare a meal. The Iroquois had a well-developed sense of hospitality even before the Gospel was announced in their villages— it was one of the natural virtues with which God had graced them.

When the Onondaga entered, Catherine set a kettle before him, and the Frenchmen came in to meet with him. After they all said grace, he told them he was on the way to Quebec with letters from the Black Robes among the Iroquois. But what piqued the curiosity of the French even more was a beautiful silver medal around his neck with the image of king Louis XIV.

"So you are in the favor of the Great Onnontiio across the water?" they asked him in Iroquois, pointing to his ornament.

"I am the Godson of the King," he answered with pride. "I was given this medal by His Majesty Himself. I am Louis Ateriata. Three years ago, I was sent by Sagochiend-agehté to Quebec after the war as a hostage to Onnontiio, and from there I went across the sea and met with the Great Chief of the French. There I was baptized and given his name."

"Aha!" said one of the Frenchman eagerly. "And what did you think of the Royal Estates? And Paris?"

Louis shrugged.

"They were not to my liking," he replied with diffidence. "Every day I longed to return to the hills of Onondaga."

The Frenchmen stared with open mouths. "It is the most splendid and luxurious city in the world!" one of them retorted.

Louis made a face and shrugged again.

Francis Xavier laughed at his guests. "So little do you know the heart of an Iroquois, my friends!"

"*None* of it was to your liking?" they pressed Louis again. He looked up toward the ceiling.

"There was one place. A place with cabin after cabin selling delicious meats roasted and on spits. So many kinds that I had never seen in all my life, not even at the greatest of our eat-all feasts."

"La Rue de la Huchette," nodded the other Frenchman.

"This place pleased me greatly," Louis concluded.

When the meal was through, the Frenchmen headed back to La Prairie while Francis and Louis put tobacco in their pipes and enjoyed a smoke. Catherine sat down near them and busied herself with her embroidery again.

"The corn is splendid," Louis said to Catherine. "God has blessed your soil."

"Indeed," she said. "it is damp but yields well."

"Do you intend to settle here?"

She looked at her husband.

"We shall see," Francis said. "I am growing fonder of it."

"It is beautiful land," Louis replied. "I should like to see more of it."

At dusk, Francis showed Louis Ateriata around. The Onondaga was particularly impressed by the lush and close-set corn, and he listened intently to Francis's description of fishing in the Tortue and the hunting in the surrounding woods, before they retired to the longhouse for evening prayers.

After a particularly refreshing night's rest, the Onondaga awoke early and walked alone in the cold mist along the river. When he returned to the longhouse, Catherine led them all in morning prayers. The duties of religion having been fulfilled, Louis gathered his things again and prepared to depart for Quebec.

Catherine handed him a leather sack. "Here is more meat for your journey. And the raspberries you relished last evening," she handed him an even larger sack of dried fruit. "I would have given you more, but I do not wish to burden you on the journey."

"I cannot take your winter stores!" he protested.

"Take them," she pleaded. "God has been good to us. And if you should come by this way on the way home to Onondaga, I shall give you the balance."

"I thank you," he said in earnest. "You have gladdened my heart."

When he at last said his goodbyes to the members of her longhouse and began on the road to Quebec, he found he could not easily forget this little band at La Prairie.

Once Louis had delivered his letters to Father François Le Mercier, the superior of the missions, he retraced his steps back to the Tortue River, where Francis helped him build a home. Others visited in the meantime, and before the winter again fell over the St. Lawrence, Louis Ateriata's cabin was joined by three more, most notably that of Paul Honoguen-hag, Francis's old Huron friend from Lorette.

A TEACHER OF GRAMMAR

1670

Father Rafeix and a new priest entered Catherine's apartment in her longhouse and shook off the cold. Looking up from her cooking, she rose to welcome them and bade them sit before the fire.

"Is Francis away?" Rafeix asked in Huron.

"He is on a hunt."

He gestured toward the other priest. "Did you have occasion at Quebec to meet a Monsieur Pierson? He came three years ago and has been teaching at the college."

She shook her head. He had a very kindly face and sincere smile.

"Father Pierson received his orders this fall," Rafeix continued, "and Father Le Mercier has decided to post him here at the mission."

"Oh!" she said joyfully. "God bless you!"

"And this," said Father Rafeix to his companion in French, "is the illustrious Catherine Gandeaktena, wife of Francis Xavier Tonsahoten. The 'Good Christian' as she is known to the Iroquois."

Pierson bowed. "It is my pleasure, Madame. Father Rafeix has praised your name from one end of the St. Lawrence to the other."

When Father Rafeix translated, she blushed and shook her head.

"We must have you both for a feast," she replied. "And we will give due honor to God for your arrival. Will you be saying the Great Prayer for Father Rafeix?"

"I fear not as yet, Madame," Pierson answered. "It would give me no greater pleasure, but I'll not be commencing my duties immediately. This winter I am to follow the hunters into the forest and study the Huron language."

When Rafeix told her what he had said, her eyes sparkled, and he did not fail to notice.

"Father Pierson perhaps does not know the great assistance our Catherine has already rendered to our order. She was the teacher of the Iroquois language to our Father Bruyas at Oneida."

"Ah! No, I did not know!" Pierson replied.

"What languages do you speak Catherine?" Rafeix asked wryly, already knowing the answer. Pierson had taught grammar at Quebec and was known for his keen linguistic interests.

"Erie, Oneida, and Huron."

He repeated his question and her answer to Pierson. "But Erie we have no use for," he added, "as the nation has been destroyed and only a few captives remain among the Iroquois. In any case, the principles of all three languages are largely the same. He who learns Huron and Iroquois can make himself understood by all of these tribes."

"Father," Catherine interposed, "it is not necessary that Father Pierson go into the woods with the hunters. We have plenty of room here in our longhouse. Ask him if he wishes to spend the winter here."

He did so.

"Madame is too kind!" Father Pierson replied, touched by her hospitality. "But a poor Walloon who knows not their manners and ways, whose nose will be ever in a book and his conjugations? Would that not be a great imposition on them?"

Father Rafeix smiled.

"This cabin, good Father, is a refuge to Indian and

Frenchman alike. Were she yet wholly pagan Iroquois, she would not dare to turn you away. It will certainly be no imposition on a soul refined by grace. I will ask her, of courtesy, but she will not say any different."

He repeated Pierson's question in Huron, and she shook her head. "Staa! Staa!"

"Certainly not," he translated, adding: "It would be, in fact, a great honor and a blessing from the Master of Life for her to give shelter to a priest in their longhouse. And I will add, Father, that you will find no better caretaker and patient teacher than the one who stands before you."

"Then of courtesy, Madam," he said to her in French with a great smile, "this humble pupil accepts your gracious offer. And I will render any service I can to you and this most blessed longhouse."

As Rafeix translated, Pierson bowed deeply.

Catherine nodded in return, laughing at his obliging nature and good sense of humor.

The rest of that year, she patiently answered Father Pierson's questions and went over variation after variation of the complex Iroquoian verb. Meanwhile, hunters, travelers, and the curious continued to arrive along the banks of La Tortue. In the summer alone, seven or eight hundred Indians passed that way.

Some were simply hunting in the rich forests below the St. Lawrence. Some wanted to see for themselves this new settlement. Others, attracted to the faith of the Black Robes, sought a place where they could practice the Christian life away from the scorn of pagans and the outbursts of drunkards. They came from the Iroquois cantons, not only free Iroquois but also the captives living among them: members of the shattered Hurons, of the Neutral Nation, and of the powerful Conestogas toward the south. And from the Algonquin lands they also came, hunters and missionaries from the north and from the Ottawa tribe further up the St. Lawrence.

Whatever their motives and whatever their origin, all found in Francis and Catherine's cabin at Kentake a perfect example of traditional Iroquoian hospitality, sweetened by her natural disposition and enflamed by the burning love that sacramental grace had instilled within her. She fed them all with the gifts of God—the meat that Francis Xavier had won with his arquebus and with the fruits of the harvest which she had sown and drawn from the land. The soil yielded a bountiful crop of corn—enough to last the community two years. But far from hoarding this natural abundance, Francis and Catherine ended up giving it all to the hundreds of travelers who passed that way.

The hungry who came were fed. The discontented were consoled. The spiritually empty were filled with prayer and love of God. To those sensitive individuals and those wearied with the decline and degradation of their homeland, it seemed as if their culture had been given a new lease on life. As once Rome's glory collapsed from her decadence while the best of her language and law carried on within the Church, so too did the heirs of the Great Peacemaker find that the Master of Life could renew His beloved Iroquois people and make of them a nation of saints fit for the glories of heaven.

And the abundant graces at La Prairie were to redouble thanks to two things that were introduced to the little town that summer of 1670.

First, the increasing French and Indian settlement inspired Father Rafeix to build a proper chapel that could accommodate the needs of the growing population.

Second, was a string of beads.

W hen Francis Xavier returned to his longhouse from a walk one afternoon, Father Pierson was at the fire with Catherine.

The priest studiously put his quill to paper, and he repeated what he had just written.

"No, no," Catherine laughed, and corrected him slowly.

He raised his eyebrow. She repeated it a third time, and he crossed out what was on the page. He was catching on and could by now make himself understood, but it was slow going, as Iroquoian languages were organized along radically different lines than the Latin and French he was used to.

Meanwhile, Francis Xavier sat himself by the fire. He was less interested in grammar than whatever was in the kettle.

"Well, let us eat now, Father," Catherine said, not wishing to try her husband's patience unnecessarily.

Father Pierson led them all in saying grace in Huron, then she filled two small kettles and set them before the priest and her husband before ladling out one for herself. They talked convivially, Catherine taking the occasion to ask the priest all sorts of doctrinal and philosophical questions while Francis Xavier inquired about the chapel that Father Rafeix was building.

When they finished the meal, Catherine collected the kettles, putting hers and her husband's to the side. She then began washing Father Pierson's.

"Catherine," he addressed her imploringly.

She looked up.

"You must not wash my kettle!"

The Iroquois were typically not fastidious about their food and did not wash their kettles after a meal—it was one of the innumerable cultural adjustments that the Jesuits had to make when they were assigned to the missions.

"Oh nonsense!" Catherine smiled, ignoring him.

"Please do not—I have no wish to be an imposition."

"You French cannot eat from dirty vessels," she replied.

He shook his head. "Nor Walloons either, it seems," he corrected good naturedly.

Francis Xavier lit a pipe for himself.

"This one you shall not win, Father," he said with a nod and a smile. "Were you a mere settler, it would be difficult enough. But there is no force on earth that would allow her to pass up an act of charity for a Black Robe."

"She loves everyone tenderly," the priest replied, taking out a pipe of his own. "It is a signal grace."

Catherine blushed and shook her head.

After they had smoked a while, the priest got up to leave.

"I promised some new visitors I would pay them a call after dinner," he explained. "Before I go, however..." he reached into his pocket and pulled out a string of beads.

"In recompense for your charity," he said, placing them in Catherine's hands. "This is a most special chaplet. It is but a trifle in the eyes of the world, but if used well, it will open for you the whole treasury of heaven."

He said his goodbyes and departed.

Father Pierson never explained what he had given to her—but she later learned that it was a Chaplet of the Confraternity of the Holy Family, whose devotion was just then spreading among the French and the Hurons at Lorette.

Inspired by this new devotion, she determined to serve God even more faithfully than ever. On the sixth of May 1671, she and two other specially chosen Christian women at La Prairie, Anastasia Tegonhatsiongo and Marie Gagaouatons, were given the rare honor of enrollment in the Confraternity.

And still more travelers and settlers came.

The fame of Francis and Catherine's little settlement was

drawing not only the pious but also the merely curious—those who had little interest in the doctrines of the Black Robes and simply wanted to partake of its material goods. Catherine's cabin was as open to these as any Christian—but she did not fail in her performance of the spiritual works of mercy either. Where she found a receptive ear, she spoke of God and the necessity to be baptized. Where she found an unreceptive one, she would redouble her prayers.

Her sweet disposition and mildness seldom gave anyone cause for complaint, save on occasions when her zeal for the faith was involved. One Iroquois woman who had come to La Prairie proclaimed publicly that she showed no interest in the Prayer, and she dismissed Catherine's talk as so much nonsense.

"Then you will be burned forever," Catherine told her frankly, "because you will not listen to what is said to you for your salvation."

As she saw, however, that this woman was greatly irritated by her impetuous remark, Catherine later sought her out privately and asked pardon for having given her cause for anger.

Yet it was evident to her husband that something would have to be done about the influx of pagans at La Prairie. Francis Xavier had fallen in love with this beautiful country along the St. Lawrence, and he had no desire to see his little settlement spiral down into the same kind of liquor-ridden, decadent vice that he had left behind at Oneida and that now plagued the Algonquin missions further up the river.

So as once the Peacemaker set out the law which brought peace to the cantons of the Iroquois and created the confederacy of the longhouse, so too would the moody Huron and his neighbors have to establish a system of governance for their little settlement—a law that would enshrine the spirit of the mission that Catherine carried within her heart.

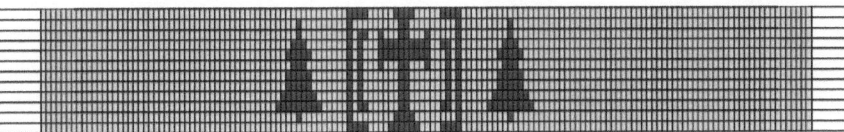

THE TWO TREES

Summer, 1671

While Father Rafeix looked on solemnly in his richly ornamented cope, Paul Honoguenhag, by now regarded as one of the stalwarts of the mission, stood and addressed the congregants.

"Today we perform a duty of the utmost importance. We have decided that this settlement here at La Prairie shall be a permanent one. We have elected to establish a means of governance among us, so that we can not only live in peace with each other in accordance with our traditions, but also regulate our mode of life in accord with the tenets of the Prayer.

"Let us then commend the matter to God, and let us offer our Mass with this intention: that He take pity upon his poor settlement, formed from the scattered nations of Canada, and that He give us wisdom to decide on these matters with prudence and love for the Prayer, without which we and all our endeavors would be lost."

Catherine looked to her husband, who nodded approvingly as Paul seated himself on the floor and began a hymn in Huron which everyone joined in singing while Father Rafeix processed up toward the altar.

Introibo ad altare Dei, he whispered.

After Mass, the elders of La Prairie debated and then selected Francis Xavier as their chief and Paul as the leader of prayer. All assembled for a grand ceremony, where Francis was formally called forward and invested with the pipe, a reed mat, and other tokens of his new office.

In his address to his countrymen, Francis Xavier spoke as an adopted Iroquois.

"In the time of the Great Peacemaker, the Five Nations made a treaty to bind themselves one to the other and end the strife that had, until then, darkened the soil with blood and caused the sun to be hidden in the sky. For many years, our fathers and grandfathers have made every effort to keep this peace. When the chiefs were in agreement, we acted with one heart, and when the chiefs were not, the fire at Onondaga was covered, each one went their own way, and still there was peace.

"We, my brothers, who have the Prayer have been accused of dishonoring the traditions of our nation.

"But what have our accusers, who style themselves the sole heirs of Deganawida, done to honor them? He brought peace between the nations. Now there is no peace even within a single longhouse. Our kinsmen, from the Eastern Door to the Western Door, murder each other for drink. They think to excuse themselves by saying 'I had no sense'—yet in so saying they convict themselves the more. For if they knew, before the drink, that this powerful medicine would cause them to become crooked and reckless, why then did they take it?

"The hunter who has lost the trail of his prey does not blindly stumble forward. He retraces his steps and searches until the path is clear once again. Our brother Christ has now given us the law of the Prayer. It is a law greater even than that of our Peacemaker, for it is for eternity, and not merely for a time. It is a law for all nations, and not merely for five. Indeed, it is so precious a thing, that if He Who Has Made All asked it of us, we should count ourselves fortunate even to utterly extinguish every last one of our beloved traditions and live as Frenchmen the rest of our days.

"But, my brothers, He does not ask it of us. Our great Jesus is content that his Iroquois remain Iroquois, save only that they love Him and abandon forever those sorceries of the demon by which they have been corrupted, and indeed by which all nations have been corrupted since our grandfather Adam ate from the forbidden tree.

"We scattered remnants, brought by many paths to the town of Kentake, are of one heart to remain. We are of one heart to uphold the Prayer. And we are of one heart to retain the customs of our people, all save those that have been spoiled by vice and our attachment to sin.

"Two trees we have planted at the entrance of our village. The first tree is drunkenness, and the second impurity. Our cabins are open to all from the Iroquois cantons who wish to settle among us. But let every man, woman, and child be warned, that they shall not cross the threshold of Kentake unless they agree to hang their vices upon these trees, and abandon them forever. Should any one dare to bring such deadly sins within the circuit of our village, he shall be turned away."

This day in the Year of Our Lord 1672 would prove more momentous than even the original formation of the League. For this new government that had begun at La Prairie would eventually command the allegiance not only of Iroquois but also Huron, Algonquin, Abenaki and other nations along the St. Lawrence who counted themselves devoted sons and daughters of the Church.

In the years to come, this mission was destined to become the capital or central fire of a new Confederacy: the Tsiatak Nihononwentsiake, the Seven Indian Nations of Canada. In its Christian life and liturgy it would serve as a shining example to all its neighboring missions. It would produce martyrs as stalwart as those of old Rome. And in its rich spiritual soil would soon grow a lily who would earn the honor of the whole world: St. Kateri Tekakwitha.

The great pagan Deganawida had left a legacy of peace that bound the five nations of the Iroquois into an earthly alliance. A sixth, the Tuscarora, would eventually join them.

But in Christ the legacy of the League would finally be perfected, by setting seven nations on the path to heaven.

⊞⊞⊞⊞ ✝ ⊞⊞⊞⊞

Father Rafeix came to speak with the newly elected chief and his wife one evening, bearing a letter in his hand from his new Superior, Father Claude Dablon.

"You have been assigned a new priest at La Prairie. I will be departing with Father Garnier to the Seneca country."

Catherine involuntarily put her hand to her mouth at the news.

Francis Xavier only nodded. "And who shall be our priest?"

"Father Jacques Fremin, who has been among the Iroquois these past years."

The war chief shook his head.

"The Seneca are intractable. Their lust is only for blood. You will get nowhere with them."

"My dear Francis, that is unbecoming of you. You know well that the Hurons at one time resisted the Gospel. And you presume against God's mercy."

"Hm," the chief replied, unconvinced. Catherine excused herself to attend to the fire.

"What of this new priest?" Francis asked. "What can we expect of him?"

"He is one of our most able missionaries. He is of high birth, most sensible and courageous."

Rafeix waited until Catherine was out of earshot and leaned close.

"You may also find him blunt and indelicate. He has the

manner of a warrior about him. On that, at least, your minds are one." Francis nodded.

"He will also prove a great ally to you with respect to the new governor. Give him his due, and I do not see any problems."

"He will have it," Francis replied warily, "on all things touching the spiritual life of the mission."

Once he had time to assess the spiritual state of his new flock—at which he was greatly pleased—Father Fremin began to prepare the most earnest Christians to make a good confession of their sins and then to receive Holy Communion.

The effects of it were noted by all.

The Annual Narrative of the mission for that year tells us that "as soon as the fire of the Blessed Sacrament had animated our new Christians, it could not be confined to themselves; the missionary fathers heard every day from their children the sentiments of their hearts, filled with the Holy Ghost."

The Indians of La Prairie, derived from twenty-two different nations, were now united in the Body of Christ. Their natural virtues, their charity and hospitality that had been exalted in Baptism were now being perfected by the Holy Sacrifice and its adorable nourishment. They became living tabernacles of their Creator, the earthly hands, feet, and mouth of their Savior.

They preached with their lives and catechized with their love. The abundant soil of La Prairie had blessed the mission with enough corn for two years, but all of it was soon given away to the hundreds of travelers that came to visit. Rare was the resident who did not attend daily Mass and evening Vespers, and who did not confess every month. The most fervent assisted at two Masses a day and confessed once a week.

The fame of La Prairie was spreading throughout Iroquoia—and those who heard tell of it had trouble believing the stories, until they came and could admire it for themselves. And many who admired—to the dismay of their tribal elders—would be so moved that they would quietly slip away from their homelands to join this new holy experiment on the banks of the St. Lawrence.

The great Mohawk warrior Togouiroui, who commanded great respect in his home country and was flush with a great victory against the Mahican, came north to hunt in the country around Chambly. There he met there a young couple from La Prairie. Impressed by what he heard of their prayers, their life, and their doctrines, he boldly defended the Christian village to the rest of the hostile Mohawk leadership, and eventually brought 42 souls out of the Iroquois country to live among the Indians of La Prairie and Lorette.

God had seen fit to make Catherine and Francis the instruments of a marvelous work in the world. And now He would call their attention away, so as to prepare a place for them in heaven.

A REMARKABLE
DETACHMENT

Late one evening in September of 1673, when Francis Xavier had been away on a hunt, Paul Honoguenhag came to see Catherine with Father Fremin.

As they walked into her cabin, she greeted them and immediately began to prepare something, but Paul immediately interrupted her and bade her sit by the fire. By his eyes she could tell that the news was not good.

"We have word from a Mohawk, just returning from the hunt." He clasped her hand, and she already knew what he was about to say. "Your husband took ill in the woods. A sickness took him away."

For a long time she stared at the ground, and no one spoke.

"Where is he now?" she asked softly.

"They are carrying him home. They will be here in a week's time."

Then she lifted her eyes to heaven, the firelight reflected in her tears.

"God has willed it," she said in anguish.

She reached behind her and pulled her shoulder mantle over her head like a veil, wiping her cheeks with the sides.

"Please Paul...Father....leave me for a while," she whispered.

"Are you certain?" Paul replied, as softly as he could.

"Yes," she whispered.

When the men left, she pulled her mantle over her face and sobbed until she fell asleep.

U nder a bright full moon, blazing through a gap in the clouds, Francis's companions were sitting quietly by the campfire, eating their meat somberly. His body lay covered and motionless upon a makeshift wooden platform.

A strange sound, a rustling and then a loud knock, sounded from the dark woods. The men turned, but saw nothing.

But Catherine saw, through her tears, a ghostly figure moving frantically in and out, closer and then farther, around them among the tree trunks.

An old witch from Oneida—one whom Catherine had not seen since she left the Iroquois country—came into her cabin.

"You have nothing left in this world now Gandeaktena," she spat. "And your husband is uneasy in the Country of Souls. You see how he hungers and longs for flesh to devour!"

The old woman pulled out a leather bag, then opened it to reveal spiky roots shaped like a carrot: water hemlock, or suicide root.

"There is nothing for you but to die now. And keep him company in the Country of Souls." She held the roots out toward Catherine. "Here!"

Catherine pushed away through the air and drew back. "I must trust in God."

"Fool!" the old woman spat. "Francis trusted your God. And see how he suffers for it? And *you* will suffer too, you will see."

The ghostly figure of Francis Xavier snaked around the trunk of a tree to a crotch in the branches, a little more than a man's height above the ground. There the hunters had left the remains of their kill—which he now set upon greedily.

"No," Catherine countered. "He will be happy with Jesus in heaven. And the Fathers and the Praying Indians of Kentake will care for me, until I join him."

"Your black robes did not care for Tonsahoten, and they will not care for thee!" the old woman fired back. "He died in the woods, without their spirit medicine. And now his soul is trapped. Go to him," she commanded. "and if you leave to me all you possess, I will fill your grave with all the goods that you will need for the afterlife, and I will leave piles of corn upon it for the journey. And all the women of Oneida will gather one night in secret, and dance the Dance of the Dead for you both."

Catherine shook her head and motioned for the old woman to leave.

"Ungrateful child! Do you think your black robes would do as much?" she spat with fury. "They will forbid it! And your souls will never journey west to the Land of Souls. They will wander the earth here forever, in search of flesh to devour!"

Just then, Catherine blinked open her eyes to the dark of her longhouse. She was all alone in her bed in the early morning, and La Prairie was still and quiet.

But her head was weighed down with a heavy, overbearing pain, and the Oneida witch's words still resounded in her ears.

When the sun rose, Catherine was early at chapel, sitting silently before the Blessed Sacrament with reddened, exhausted eyes. When Mass began, she sat through it as usual, but then she left right away without speaking to Father Fremin.

She kept to herself the next day and the one following, busying herself with her chores but not speaking much to anyone inside or outside her longhouse.

Only after three days did she finally appear at the priest's cabin, while he was at work copying a manuscript.

"Father?"

"Come in, come in."

"I am sorry for absenting myself. I have had a great deal to think about."

"No no....there is no sin in it," he reassured her. She winced suddenly and rubbed her forehead.

"Are you ill?"

"No, no...just a headache, Father."

"Ah," he replied.

"What do you need?"

"I am my own mistress now, Father. And now that I am free, I am resolved to give half of all I possess to the poor, and the other half to the church of the Blessed Virgin. It is sufficient for me to enough to clothe myself. For my food, and for all else, the Providence of God will make provision."

The priest was amazed to hear such a bold declaration from someone so recently stricken with grief. But notwithstanding the earnestness in her voice, Fremin shook his head.

"Dearest. You have lost your sole means of support. I cannot condone this immoderate fervor. You will make yourself the poorest woman of La Prairie, and have need of everyone else's charity to even survive."

Surprised, she blinked and and said nothing.

"Do you understand?" he said.

"I do," she said slowly, though not very convincingly.

"Do nothing for now," he directed bluntly. "Let us wait until after the funeral, and we will talk about it then."

"After?" she asked, distractedly, rubbing her forehead again.

"Yes. After." he said with greater force. She was showing a curious resistance to his advice—a quality he had never seen in her before. But she nodded, thanked him, and began the walk back to her longhouse.

The hunting party returned to La Prairie a few days later. As they approached, Catherine veiled herself with her mantle and steeled herself to receive her husband's body. She stood at the edge of the village and prayed silently.

But there was no corpse being borne by the men—and they were joking raucously. Then she heard a familiar laugh and she saw Francis Xavier walking among his fellow hunters. Teary-eyed she ran to him and threw her arms around his neck while he looked about him in confusion. The other men laughed, but then exchanged puzzled glances with Francis.

"Francis! They said you were dead!" Paul shouted, walking toward the party.

"Dead? Who said that?" Francis repeated.

"The Mohawk!"

As the understanding dawned on him, he dropped his kit and wrapped a strong arm around his wife. "I'm alright! I am alive!"

He wiped her cheek with his hand. "I'm alright. I'm alright."

She finally relaxed and took in a deep, wheezing breath, resting her hand on his chest.

"Come..." he reassured her. "Let's get you home."

Early in the next joyous morning, with only a dim light in the longhouse, Catherine emerged in an ecstasy from her husband's side under the warm blankets. The slight autumn chill washed over her bare skin, and she delighted in the sensation. She wrapped a skirt around herself, put on her overdress, then sat down and pulled up her leggings. She revived the dying fire at the center of the longhouse, set some fresh deer meat to roast on a spit and finally gazed with deep affection at her Francis in the dim light, still sleeping soundly beneath the bear skins.

But as she meditated on the last several days, a somber thought entered, unbidden, into her reverie.

He had been restored to her, yes. But only for a while. And the grief she had felt over his passing surely she would feel again when he succumbed to the common doom of all mankind. The joy she felt at his return—real and heartfelt as it was—was only a temporary one.

She lingered on the thought, though it did not dampen her joy as much as temper it with a grave somberness. And as time passed, she sat staring at the fire.

When Francis finally arose, dressed, and kissed her on the forehead, he saw that she had taken out her finest jewelry—a girdle and bracelets of wampum that she now wore on the great festivals of the Church. He gestured to the finery.

"Why did you take these out?"

"I had an evil dream," she answered, "and I promised to give away everything the poor. But Father Fremin stopped me."

He smirked. "For once, it is my wife who has acted impetuously!"

"I have. And now—" she began. "Well—even now that you're back, I can't really think of them as mine anymore. What I promised to the poor is just as much theirs as if the news of your death were true."

He looked solemnly at her but said nothing.

"We have been very blessed Francis. I thought I lost you in this world forever, and then our good Jesus gave you back to me again. I have been blessed with this cabin, with this settlement, with these ornaments, and especially with you. But what a true pity it would be if we waited for death to detach ourselves from these wonderful things, only to need purging of them in the fires of Purgatory!"

"Mmm," he nodded at the theological truth of it, more than what she was leading to.

"I still have this girdle and these bracelets. And you have your necklace and your war-belt of wampum. What if we were to make an offering to God of all these, so that we learn the better to depend upon Him alone?"

The proud man's face hardened, and he felt a flash of resentment at the thought of being stripped of those emblems of his authority and prowess.

It was a great shame among the Iroquoian peoples to show any excessive love for goods. Among them a man unwilling to part with any object could be coerced by his peers into surrendering it with the humiliating phrase: "Thou lovest it." So Catherine had an easy means of procuring her husband's agreement—but she scorned to use it. Instead, out of love for Francis and especially for his immortal soul, she simply turned to pack up her own precious items—saying nothing, but pleading her case by her good example and her appeal to his highest principles.

He watched her for several minutes. *How much I had missed her on the hunt, and what a pure and wonderful joy it had been to pass the night in each others' embrace as the moon wheeled above. What would I do without her?*

"Collect my necklace and my war-belt," he said finally, "and we shall both make a present of them to the Fathers."

After all was collected, they walked to the wooden chapel, their greatest worldly treasures in hand, piquing the curiosity of their neighbors in the longhouse and the village. A small group of people followed them in.

The Blessed Sacrament was exposed on the candle-lit altar, so everyone who came in dropped to their knees. Father Fremin was kneeling at the back of the chapel in his cassock. He had intended to go into the sacristy to vest for Benediction, but lingered instead among those who were already praying there and those who came to watch.

As they arrived at the altar rail, Francis and Catherine dropped to both knees before the Sacrament, and bowed their heads. They spent a short moment in prayer, and then Francis turned to his wife. She placed her wampum beads in his arms, atop his. Then, with all the wampum they owned, Francis rose solemnly and stepped forward into the sanctuary. Gently he laid their valuables on the first step, then genuflected on both knees again and returned to his wife at the altar rail.

They sat in silence for a moment, and then Catherine spoke aloud:

"Four years ago, my God, I gave Thee my body and soul and the greater part of my possessions. Here is what remains to me. I give it to Thee with all my heart. Thou hast given us everything—so what can I ask more of Thee? Unless it be that Thou takest me myself, from this moment, to be with Thee?"

Francis Xavier solemnly offered his own similar dedication. They then crossed themselves, stood up, and knelt in a less prominent spot in the nave to hear Mass. In the silence that followed, a few of their neighbors wept tears of joy at Catherine's piety.

Father Fremin was moved greatly as well. He whispered to those near him:

"Without a doubt God will hear this virtuous woman!"

A SECOND CHAPEL

October 21, 1673
Feast of St. Ursula

The next day the October sun was burning unusually brightly as Catherine, Anastasia, and the other women were on the ground out in the field, picking the very last of the cranberries and telling stories to pass the time. An old Lenape woman named Marie, who had long ago been adopted by the Iroquois, was telling her grandchildren the legend of the Yaquahi or mastodon among her people.

"...and He Who Has Made All saw that to lose this meat would be a great misfortune to the Lenape people, who could not survive without it. Thus, He thought to himself: 'Where the blood of the mammoth lies on the ground, I will make a berry to grow. It will be red as the meat of the monster, and it will sustain the race of the Lenape for as long as they endure in these lands.' And just by thinking so, He made the cranberry to rise out of the ground."

The girls then pestered their poor grandmother with questions. Catherine smiled as she wiped her brow with her arm. She had not been feeling right the last few days and was perhaps already coming down with a fever, but she was well enough to pick berries. Well enough, that is, for a cool October day in the field and not an unseasonably hot one. But she was here now, and didn't wish to complain.

"Marie," she said, "when I was a little girl, I remember when the River Indians and the Conestoga came to trade at my village at Gentaienton. Were these your kinsmen?"

Marie smiled. "No, not mine. My kinsmen are the Minsi, in our language—the upriver people. We traded with the Dutch in Albany. Those who long ago traded with your people were the Unami—the downriver people, with the Swedes and the Andaste."

Catherine meant to continue with another question but trailed off and shut her eyes, as a pain was steadily increasing in her head. She put her basket down and rubbed her brow as the girls began asking questions of their grandmother again.

Within the next few minutes, the pain became hard to bear. Catherine stood up somewhat dizzily and nearly fell.

"I'm sorry—" she interrupted, "I feel ill..." and started walking slowly back to the village. Anastasia came to her side and steadied her.

"Come, Catherine."

They walked side-by-side together back to her longhouse as she strained against the intense pain.

Anastasia helped her onto her cot. "Rest now dear."

She noticed on Catherine's face an odd, and quite alarming, expression, something like the irrational joy of madness. Her mouth had opened wide and she stared skyward.

"As I have prayed," Catherine said, looking at her and past her at the same time. "My desire shall soon be fulfilled."

Anastasia did not understand, and now she really began to worry.

"Rest," she repeated, and covered Catherine with a bear skin before she ran to find the men.

⊞⊞⊞⊞ ✝ ⊞⊞⊞⊞

Arriving by her bedside, Francis Xavier and Father Fremin were pleased to see her awake and alert. With great affection, they encouraged her and asked her what was wrong. But she answered distractedly, almost as if the suffering she was enduring was happening to someone else.

"I want to go to heaven," she said impatiently. "I want to go to heaven."

Francis Xavier kept vigil by her bedside, ministering to her while everyone in the village came to check on the beloved mother of the mission. She spoke not a word of her sufferings, neither to her husband or to any of her visitors. Instead, her very agonies filled her with a joy that was wonderful to behold and that made a deep impression on all who saw her.

Animated by a great love of God, Catherine's sick-room served as another chapel, a spiritual place where people came to pray rather than engage in the pleasantries of conversation. Her fellow Indians and the French crowded around her section of the longhouse to pray their beads, to make other acts of devotion, or simply to speak about God—throughout the entire day, and often through a good part of the night. A whole octave passed in this way, a week of spiritual preparation not only for Catherine but for Francis Xavier and the whole village.

On the eighth day, Father Fremin entered the longhouse, greeted Francis Xavier and then approached his wife's bedside.

"How do you feel, Catherine?"

She smiled and nodded, avoiding the question entirely. "Have you come to pray with me Father?" she said as brightly as possible.

"Indeed I have," he replied, taking his handwritten Huron prayer-book out of his satchel.

"I am glad," she nodded. "It is all I wish to do."

"You have been given a great grace, Catherine," he replied. "And you will see—once you are better, you will be able to attend the chapel again."

She raised her eyebrows with an indifferent expression.

"You do not wish to pray in the chapel?" he said with surprise.

"It is not that I don't wish it, Father. I just want to go to heaven. That is all. I want to go to heaven."

Father Fremin looked up at Francis Xavier, who returned a worried glance.

"In its own good time, Catherine. But only as God wills, not you or I."

She nodded.

"As God wills. But I have asked two great favors of Him. To die in peace, and to die with all the Sacraments."

The priest said nothing for a moment, but he saw that his spiritual daughter was losing her interest in this world.

"Do you wish the Last Rites, Catherine?" he asked.

She nodded. The gravity of her request hung in the air for a moment.

"Very well," he said. "You shall have them. But first, pity your poor father and let us pray God that you regain your health."

He turned to the page in the prayer-book and began to recite the Huron prayer for health. Like all the Indians of La Prairie, Catherine had it committed to memory. Dutifully and with great piety she said the words along with Fremin.

Yet after the prayer concluded, she looked up to the heavens and sighed. "It has been impossible for me to say from the Heart what I have just uttered from the lips."

"Oh?" Father Fremin asked.

"Why ask to remain on earth, since God is calling me to Heaven?"

He glanced up at Francis Xavier again, who shook his head almost imperceptibly and then poked at the fire with a grave expression.

"Very well," he said, rising and replacing the book into its satchel. "Let me get my stole and the oils."

That evening, Father Fremin gave the Last Sacraments of the Church to Catherine Gandeaktena. And shortly afterward, she entered into a state that was midway from this world and midway toward the next, where the final battle for her soul would take place.

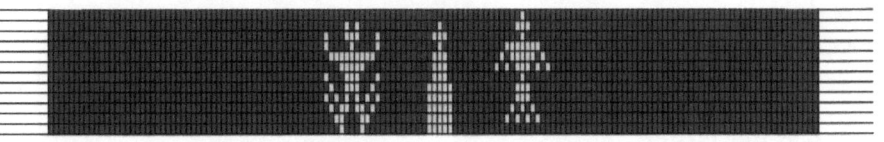

EIGHT DAYS OF DELIRIUM

In the long-lost town of Gentaienton, Catherine stood before the head *agoiander*, who brandished a sharp stick.

"And you, girl?"

She shook her head tensely. The great Annenraes was bound and tied to the stake.

"You bring shame upon us, girl! Shame! Our whole nation will burn!"

All the women hissed and jeered at Catherine.

"Burn him, girl!" one screamed. "Burn Annenraes! Or the Cats shall perish from the earth!"

She kept shaking her head, and tried to retreat backwards toward her cabin, but at her back were a half dozen strong arms behind her that pushed her forward.

The *agoiander* held up a dark firebrand, its tip glowing red and searing hot from the fire.

"Take it! Burn him!" she commanded.

She tried to wrestle away from her countrymen, but someone seized her right arm and forced it forward.

"TAKE IT!" the old woman glared imperiously. She shifted her hand higher up on the iron, and tried to force it into Catherine's hand. Catherine made a tight fist, refusing to take it.

"TAKE IT!!" the Eries screamed out in unison.

Catherine struggled and kicked but could not free her arm or move away. Unable to do anything else, she relaxed her grip, and her fingers closed around the brand.

"BURN HIM!" the crowd roared in delight.

She looked up at Annenraes—but it was not Anneraes. In the great captain's place, already partly burned and bloodied, was her father.

Catherine cried out, digging in her heels and pushing herself backwards, but a wall of Eries pushed hard on her back and shoulders. She tried to writhe around them, but there were too many.

"BURN HIM!" a young warrior yelled into her ear. She dropped the brand, her throat tense, and fought with all her strength to get away from the crowd.

"Fool, girl!" the woman elder cried over her struggles. "Do you think you can save your father from this fate? Do you think you can see him again? You are in the Prayer, and he died in the devil! You will never be together again!"

Catherine shook her head, tears streaming from her eyes.

"You are about to die! And if you die in the Prayer, you will never see your father again! From your Christian heaven you will watch him burn in a fire worse than that of the Iroquois—for all eternity!"

Catherine cried out in heartbroken pain, dropped to her knees and tried to crawl away through her countrymen's legs.

"Give up the Prayer, girl!! Die with your father, and all of your kin!"

A woman's hand suddenly wrapped around her arm and pulled her out of the plaza. "Go! Go!" her mother's voice rang in her ears. But her limbs were heavy, and she fought through the sluggishness to run as quickly as she could toward the gate.

"Catherine," she unexpectedly heard her father calling her Christian name. The women of Gentaienton laughed and jeered.

Catherine struggled to turn around, but her limbs were stiff and unresponsive. Though tears and clenched fists, she willed every ounce of strength toward her motionless legs, but they refused to respond.

Suddenly she heard strong male voice:

"*Our Father, Who Art in heaven...*"— the voice was familiar, but it was not her father's.

"*...Thy will be done, on earth as it is in heaven...*" As the prayer continued in a chorus of voices, she relaxed her fists and let out a deep breath.

"*...and deliver us from evil. So be it.*"

And then she was no longer in Gentaienton, but in her cabin at La Prairie.

Anastasia, Marie Gagaouatons, and many others were kneeling around her bed, with Francis Xavier leading them in the rosary. "*Hail Mary full of grace, the Lord is with Thee. Blessed art Thou amongst women, and blessed is the fruit of Thy womb, Jesus.*" The chorus continued the *Ave*, and he smiled as she blinked at him, though his eyes were red with worry.

By the second *Ave*, Catherine was softly reciting the prayer along with everyone else, and she continued to participate in the Rosary until it was concluded. Her friends came up to her bedside smiling and happy she was lucid again, and they assured her of their prayers.

When at last Francis and Catherine were alone, he gave her a cup of water and admitted frankly, "We nearly despaired of your speaking again."

"I have not been myself," she replied. "Whenever I close my eyes, there are new torments."

"You are awake now, and I am here," he reassured her. "And we are praying for you."

"Thank you, Francis," she said warmly. "Thank you."

He sat at the top of their bed and placed her head in his lap, then caressed her black hair. They sat in silence for a few moments.

"I am afraid, Francis. I am very afraid. May we pray some more?"

Though fatigued now with his long vigil, he reached for his rosary and nodded.

A baby cried, sharp and piercing, and Catherine opened her eyes to a familiar old longhouse in Oneida and a child lying next to her. Filled with intense joy, she cradled its warmth in her arms and put it to her breast, as her old shame was blown away like a wisp upon a warm summer wind. Every dismal thought, every worry or trouble or pain disappeared in that moment of overwhelming love for her child. In an ecstatic revelry, she wept in relieved tears, overcome by the baby's warmth, the softness of its skin, and its tender and delicate movements, as Francis Xavier slept quietly beside them both.

Reeling with happiness, she drank in every detail of its tender skin and its fine joints and the wispy hairs on its head. Its feeling on her breast, as she nourished it.

But as Catherine looked toward the longhouse door, she saw standing there, in the flickering red glow of an ember fire, the witches of Oneida.

"No baby for thee, barren Cat!"

She unlatched the baby from her breast and clutched it rigidly to herself as it cried out in hunger.

"Barren Cat! Barren Cat!" they screamed over the wailing of the baby.

She shifted over to her husband and began to shake him awake with her leg. "Francis! Francis!"

But her husband's body lay still. There, by the side of his mouth against the floor, was a dark green liquid like bile. His cold eyes stared forward at nothing.

"He's dead, Cat!" the witches taunted, holding up two medicine bags. "Dead! As dead as your womb!"

Catherine felt a sudden spasm in her belly. She looked down—blood was pooling beneath her, and she clenched her legs together.

"All your kittens are ours now!"

One of the witches held up a tendon-like string, dripping with blood, with swellings like scarlet eggs all along its length. Catherine reached out to grab it, but one of the women had already snuck around behind her. The witch snatched the baby from Catherine's arms as the others howled with demonic laughter.

"You want this one back, Cat? You want it? Curse your Jesus who made you barren! Curse him and get back your kitten! Otherwise, to the stake he goes! To the stake!"

Catherine screamed.

"Catherine!" the strong voice of Francis Xavier filled the room, as the longhouse and the witches faded from sight.

She turned her face to him, but her puzzled eyes still darted wildly.

"Catherine?" he asked again. "Can you hear me?" Her pupils locked onto his and she sat up. Tears began streaming down her face as she buried her head in his shoulder.

"Pray with me, Francis! Pray with me!"

A few days later, as a soft rain drenched the lands along the St. Lawrence, Father Fremin stopped by their longhouse.

"Is she any better?"

The warrior took his pipe out of his mouth and shook his head. His hand was trembling slightly, but the priest pretended not to notice.

"She is still delirious and being tormented by dreams and demons. She wakes only to pray. My heart tells me that she will not recover."

"Hmm," the priest replied. "I would not gainsay the mercy of God even now. But perhaps the devils are vying for her soul."

Francis nodded gravely. He stood up and paced toward the door and back again, while the two sat in silence for several minutes.

"Father," he stated boldly, "I dare not leave her side. But there is something God calls me to do before the end."

Fremin nodded. "Go. I will stay with her. I will summon you immediately if anything should happen."

The warrior put on his outer cloak slowly while looking at his wife, as if rethinking his decision. But he finally headed into the rain with determination.

The priest watched her for an hour, monitoring the restlessness of her sleep through the pattering sounds on the bark roof and the low rumble of thunder.

Just as he took out his breviary to pray None, her eyes suddenly opened and she sat up.

"I cannot understand you!" she cried in Oneida amidst tears, "I cannot understand you!"

Fremin quickly put his breviary away.

"Catherine?"

She was staring forward, not at him.

"Catherine!" he tried again.

Her eyes then began to cast around, darting frantically from everything to nothing.

"Can no one understand them?" she cried in anguish.

"Catherine, can you hear me?" Fremin called louder.

"Father!" she cried, still looking around the room.

"I am here!"

"Father!"

"Here, Catherine! I am here!"

"They are burning them, Father! They are burning them! Pray for them, Father!"

Before long, the longhouse was crowded with Francis and Catherine's friends. Francis had visited them all, and invited them to join him in a great feast, similar to the ones the pagan Iroquois employed to snatch a loved one's life back from a grave illness.

As he saw the longhouse fill, Father Fremin had some cause to worry that Francis was backsliding under the stress of his wife's illness. But he also trusted the Huron warrior, and held his peace. Wisely, as it turns out, for when everyone had finally arrived, Francis addressed the crowd as follows:

"Formerly, before we were Christians, the maladies of our beloved threw us into the utmost distress. We therefore followed the customs of our ancestors and made use of superstitions in order to cure our sick. But now we are Christians, and we pray. So instead, we invoke the names of Jesus and of Mary, and we ask of them a cure. That is why I now pray you all to intercede for my sick wife and to say the rosary for her. But—if our loved ones yet die, we also comfort ourselves in the hope of seeing them again in Heaven. So let us then say our beads for Catherine who is in her agony, before beginning our feast."

Francis looked toward Father Fremin and gestured deferentially. The priest nodded, and reached into his cassock for his rosary.

Catherine was all alone in her longhouse at La Prairie, her breath misting in the frigid air. Everything was covered in an eerie, unnatural darkness. There was no fire lit, but the walls threw shadows that had leaked in from a bright conflagration outside.

"Aiiiiiiiiii!" a terrible scream of pain, almost as that of an animal, lingered outside the longhouse walls. It went on en-

tirely too long, then it broke into the sound of a woman cry-
ing in exhausted heaves through a hoarsened throat. Catherine's hands trembled as she threw her mantle over her head
and covered her ears, but she heard another desperate scream
from a different woman, before a howl of cackles and laughter
drowned it out out.

"Please, Lord!" Catherine pleaded.

Just then, Father Bruyas threw open the door of the longhouse and ran to Catherine. There was blood on his cassock.
"The demon has taken Kentake! The sun has grown dark in
the sky and the two trees have fallen!" he cried in anguish. "I
have need of you!"

She shook her head.

"There are Erie captives! Come!" he said more forcefully. A man's chilling scream pierced through the longhouse
wall—a voice Catherine knew from her earliest days. She
shuddered and shook her head, unable to move.

"You must, Catherine! You must save these poor souls!"

"I am afraid, Father!!" she cried out through tears, "I am
afraid!"

Behind the priest, a shadow appeared, silhouetted against
the fire beyond. The great and terrible Iroquois warrior
Aharihon approached the open door, his head a writhing mass
of snakes. He was brandishing an iron in his right hand and
the tip glowed red-hot.

"Come Catherine!" Bruyas said sternly. "Or they will die
damned!"

She tried to slink back further into the longhouse, but
her limbs refused to move, as if just waking from a nightmare.
The shadowy Aharihon was now at the priest's back, ready to
plunge the fire-brand into her face.

"In the name of God, get up!" Bruyas shouted, holding
his right hand toward her.

"*Jesous, tagitenra!*" she cried out, and forced her sluggish
muscles forward to grasp the priest's arm.

He pulled her forward.

There was now only a clear, bright sunlight. The terrors and screams had all vanished, and the birds were singing in delight.

"Well done, Catherine," Father Bruyas said proudly. "Well done." He led her to the plaza and its central cross, and then bowed reverently and retreated to his cabin.

There, at the base of the cross, stood a man with a radiant, noble though unfamiliar face. He was vested as a Huron of many centuries ago, but wearing a *gustoweh*, a traditional Iroquoian cap, and holding in his hands a belt of wampum.

"Come, my daughter," he said, and her heart danced at his voice. As she approached, she saw that his *gustoweh* was not made of ash wood and turkey feathers, but of the thorny branches of honey locust that grew in her native land.

"My daughter: through you I bring a new peace unto my beloved nations. A new longhouse among them will now arise—a new confederacy, where all the many hearths will live as one family, one household, and one nation."

"And you, faithful one, will complete the work of Jikonhsase who tamed the wild Hiawatha. It is your cabin at La Prairie that will ever be remembered as its home and its hearth. A five-fold peace was given to your people many years ago. It yet endures, and in the coming years it shall even increase and be made six. But as such it will forever remain imperfect—a thing of this world.

"But the peace that I now bring is not of this world, and it will endure to the end of time. Be evermore at peace, Catherine Gandeaktena of the Erie, Mother of Nations!"

The Great Peacemaker handed her a great wampum belt—a belt of seven nations centered on a cross. As he handed it to her, she saw the wounds in his hands and his feet, and as she lifted her eyes to thank him, his holy face was already transforming into its true form.

"Catherine?" a calm voice called through the gentle pat-
ter of rain on the bark roof.

"Catherine?"

Her eyes blinked open. Francis Xavier was again kneeling
by her bed, a tear running down his warrior's cheek, and his
hand grasped tightly around his rosary. Behind him, Father
Fremin smiled and placed his beads back in his cassock.

"Francis," she whispered with a great relief.

His grizzled face warmed with a little worried smile.

"Do not worry for me, my heart," she said to reassure him.

"You have your wish," he said, fighting not to choke on
his words.

"Yes," she smiled.

She shifted in her place, but had little strength left.

"Keep your promises," she said, "Refrain from drink, and
persevere in the Faith."

He nodded manfully.

"I will, dearest."

"Francis," she said at last very slowly, with devotion. She
reached up and softly touched his cheek, then fought to shift
her exhausted body closer to his own. Her breathing was la-
bored and came out in heavy wheezes. But her reddened eyes
now sparkled with a great joy. She stared with a childlike innocence at Francis's face, a slight smile in her open mouth.

There was an immense radiance and an innocent wonder
in her eyes—and she gazed at him with an outpouring of pure
love, like Eve newly brought to the side of Adam.

"Rest, dear one. Rest," Francis whispered back, gently
taking her hand and placing it on her breast. Another tear
bathed his cheek, but she did not see it. She had closed her
eyes, and with a smiling and angelic face, fell into a long,
sweet sleep.

Nine days later, on November the sixth, in the year of Our Lord Sixteen Hundred and Seventy-Three, Catherine Gandeaktena of the Erie Nation, the good Christian, the Pillar of the Faith, and the Mother of the Poor, perished to the mortal world.

EPILOGUE:
A NEW CUSTOM

B efore the council fire of La Prairie, the grieving war chief
Francis Xavier Tonsahoten stood to address Paul Honoguenhag and the other elders.

"It has been our custom," he began, "to give away the be-
longings of the dead to relatives and friends, in order that they
may lament them. And also to set up tombs for them, on which
we paint whatever beasts and birds served as their 'Masters of
Life' when the departed walked the earth.

"But we ought to adhere to these customs no longer," he
said sternly. "which bring no advantage to the dead. For my
part, then, my desire is to array the body of the deceased with
the very best of what she possessed, since she will rise again in
Christ one day. And whatever remains of what once belonged
to her, I intend to distribute as alms to the poor, that they pray
for her soul."

Remembering the heroic donation that his wife almost
made when she had heard of his death, Francis was now in
a position to make good on it—in such a way that Father
Fremin could not object.

Through her death Catherine had fulfilled her great desire: to be left only with the clothes on her back, and to rely
for all else on the Providence of God. Her remaining wealth
on earth—which amounted to 300 French livres—was dis-
tributed among all the poor of La Prairie, along with Francis's
solemn charge: "Pray for the dead woman."

All the Indians of the mission, drawn together by Christ from over 20 nations, and the local French, joined Francis Xavier in a Requiem Mass for their beloved Catherine. They all spoke highly of her virtues, as of one they believed to be enjoying the bliss of heaven.

All who attended the bark chapel of La Prairie that day saw the precious strings of wampum hung loosely by the altar, which had been consecrated to it only a few weeks before.

Having read the Gospel of the *Requiem*, Father Jacques Fremin removed his black maniple, laid it gently on the Missal, and turned to address the crowd.

"God has afflicted this mission," he said. "by taking from it its foundress Catherine Gandeaktena. It is truly a great affliction. For the poor have lost their mother, the Christians have lost their example, and the Indians and the French have both lost their well-beloved. She has left this chapel heir to the ornaments of her youth, and these she has made all the more precious through the consecration that she made of them during her lifetime."

In the years to come, these ornaments of purple and white wampum would be affixed to the beams of the church and used to decorate the altar frontal—a fitting visual reminder of the marine byssus and purple of the valiant woman of Proverbs.

And the customs observed at Catherine's funeral formed the mission's Christian Iroquois culture for decades to come. Three years after her death, the entire mission moved a few miles upriver to better farming lands at the Sault St. Louis. There, it would gain greater spiritual fame as the garden of piety that would cultivate the Lily of the Mohawks.

Father Fremin believed that Catherine Gandeaktena died in baptismal innocence; that she had reached so exalted a state of virtue, and so wonderful a purity of heart, that nothing remained for her to atone for in the next life. Nor does he seem to have been alone in this belief. For when the cemetery of

La Prairie was finally moved in 1689, the Indians of the Sault and the French settlers contended over who would retain her relics.

Only one year before that translation, in the winter of 1688, Francis Xavier Tonsahoten, the Father of the Faithful, had gone to his own final rest. He had never remarried, and he faithfully kept his wife's dying wish, persevering in the Catholic Faith to the very end.

And it was said that when, in moments of weakness, his passionate and moody nature reasserted itself, he could be quieted in a moment by the mere name of his beloved Catherine.

A COMMEMORATION OF CATHERINE GANDEAKTENA

(for private use only)

NOVEMBER 6TH

She hath considered a field and bought it; with the fruit of her hands she hath planted a vineyard.

V/. She hath opened her hand to the needy,
R/. and stretched out her hand to the poor.

Let us pray.

O God, we thank Thee for the graces Thou hast bestowed on Thy servant Catherine, whom Thou called from slavery to be the mother of Christians and pillar of faith for the Iroquois. Humbly we pray that, if it be Thy will, her name be soon raised to the dignity of the altars. We ask this through Christ our Lord Thy Son, who liveth and reigneth with Thee and the Holy Spirit, world without end, Amen.

www.ingramcontent.com/pod-product-compliance
Lightning Source LLC
Chambersburg PA
CBHW031606260626
47154CB00020B/1646